Praise for *Run*

'It's a cliché to say that there's something for everyone in this book but there just is.'
Books+Publishing

'These are stories that often inhabit a gritty, substantive "rural dreamscape" that explores the darker, disconcerting ways that Australia's remote geography and haunted history imprint themselves on our collective psyche.'
The Advertiser

'The characters were so vividly drawn that I entered every story completely.'
Imbi Neeme, winner of the 2019 Penguin Literary Prize

'Rural Australia is a dangerously neglected part of our national consciousness – Margaret Hickey populates it with stories that are lively, entertaining and authentic.'
Martin Flanagan

Margaret Hickey is an award-winning author, playwright and teacher from North East Victoria. She has a PhD in Creative Writing and is deeply interested in rural lives and communities. She is the author of *Cutters End*, *Stone Town* and *Broken Bay*. Her latest novel, *The Creeper*, was released in August 2024.

RURAL DREAMS

ALSO BY MARGARET HICKEY

Cutters End
Stone Town
Broken Bay
The Creeper

MARGARET HICKEY

RURAL DREAMS

STORIES FROM THE BUSH

PENGUIN BOOKS

UK | USA | Canada | Ireland | Australia
India | New Zealand | South Africa | China

Penguin Books is part of the Penguin Random House group of companies
whose addresses can be found at global.penguinrandomhouse.com

Penguin
Random House
Australia

First published by MidnightSun Publishing in 2020
This paperback edition published by Penguin Books in 2025

Copyright © Margaret Hickey 2025

The moral right of the author has been asserted.

Cover images © Ondrej Prosicky/iStock.com and Leah-Anne Thompson/Shutterstock.com
Cover design by Christabella Designs © Penguin Random House Australia Pty Ltd
Author photograph © Charlotte Guest
Typeset in 12.5/17.5 pt Adobe Garamond Pro by Midland Typesetters, Australia

Printed and bound in Australia by Griffin Press, an accredited
ISO AS/NZS 14001 Environmental Management Systems printer

A catalogue record for this
book is available from the
National Library of Australia

ISBN 978 1 76135 109 9

penguin.com.au

MIX
Paper | Supporting
responsible forestry
FSC® C018684

We at Penguin Random House Australia acknowledge that Aboriginal and Torres Strait Islander
peoples are the Traditional Custodians and the first storytellers of the lands on which we live
and work. We honour Aboriginal and Torres Strait Islander peoples' continuous connection
to Country, waters, skies and communities. We celebrate Aboriginal and Torres Strait Islander
stories, traditions and living cultures; and we pay our respects to Elders past and present.

*To the country kids who think about moving
back home, and to those who never left.*

CONTENTS

SATURDAY MORNING

It's never easy to get up on a Saturday morning, but it's harder still when it's early, minus one degree outside and you've got a new girlfriend snuggled up in bed. She looks like a little bird, he thinks; small and neat, mouth pursed like she's about to speak.

He lies there for a moment, hands behind his head, trying to make out the first feeble rays of light through the window. They're not there yet. Not at this time of year.

He closes his eyes for a second, feels sleep race towards him. It would be so easy to stay, easy to turn on his side, curl up beside Jess and put his hand up her top; feel her warm skin and quiet breathing.

Nothing more than a phone call would do it. Gastro – food poisoning, the usual code for *can't be stuffed*.

He fumbles about the room trying not to wake her and when he farts, it's in the bathroom. Early days yet.

He's quietly cursing whatever it is he's doing, even as he pulls on his jeans and t-shirt. It's cold here – but where he's going it's colder still. He locates his beanie. Last week he forgot it and the wind nearly blew his brains out.

The house is asleep and the blokes he shares with won't be up till almost midday. They got home with Jess late last night from band practice and they drank and sang till early in the morning. Not so long ago in fact. They thought he was mad for not joining them.

But while he likes a drink, he's not musical, and besides, there's always the morning to think of.

The kitchen is a pigsty, but he doesn't mind. Not really. He finds a bowl in the sink and gives it a rinse, finds a clean teaspoon. There's not much by the way of food in the cupboard, but he fits six Weet-Bix in the bowl and piles on the sugar. If this was his family home, there would be the smell of his father's bread baking and a warm afterglow from the wood fire. Not here. He jumps up and down, gives the milk a cursory sniff and eats as quietly and quickly as he can.

He looks around. It's alright for a share house, he's been in worse. Next year, once he finishes engineering, he'll be off overseas backpacking. Maybe with Jess. London, Europe, Asia, however long the money lasts.

He knows it's kind of boring, but mostly he'd like to go to Ireland; see the cliffs there, drive down those little roads. Jess would like to go to Shanghai but he's not so sure.

He brushes his teeth and takes a jug of lukewarm water outside, pours it over the windscreen. The ice crackles and melts.

In the distance, he hears a siren – its rise and fall a desolate wail. In the early hours the city is dense and dark – it's a time for headlights and whispers, for taxis bringing home the dejected, the rejected and the newly arrived.

He chucks his bag in the back of the old car and revs the engine. It's noisy and right outside the bedroom window. The blind whips open and Jess's face appears, as he half hoped it would. Her brown hair sticks to the sides of her flushed face; she's bleary with warmth and sleep and wine. She puts on a sad face and waves to him. He puts on a sad face and waves back. In response she shrugs and pulls the blind down fast. He backs out of the driveway and turns onto the street.

He's been with her for three months, but he doesn't fully get her. She's his first real girlfriend and he thinks he might love her but he's not sure. He feels proud of her sharp intelligence and the way people are drawn to her, but the endless talking exhausts him. Jess likes causes and heavy discussions deep into the night. She claims that he is her rock and that he grounds her, but sometimes when she says that, when her teeth are stained from red wine like she's just bitten the head off a possum, he feels slightly afraid. For the most part they are good together, they don't fight, and he finds the sex deeply satisfying. He probably does love her.

But she can't understand this, this need of his to leave early on Saturday mornings every week from May till September. It wrecks their Friday nights, she says, hinders their weekend plans and prevents him from attending events important to her and their friends.

Take today, for instance. His roommates, friends since O week, have been invited to play a gig at a pub in Fitzroy. That's a paid gig. Offers like that don't come around very often. Not for bands like *Werribee don't stink no more.*

A crowd is important at events like this. They would need to invite *all* their friends. Someone drew up a list. Someone else poured drinks. Would they invite their parents? No – because they'd bring the mood down. Yes – because they'd be the most likely to shout drinks and then the management would be pleased. Parents, tick.

More discussion. And more. There was a slight change in the kitchen air when he said he couldn't come. A not altogether pleasant one. He protested: it wouldn't mean much if he wasn't there – besides helping to move equipment and drive the truck he wasn't at all integral to their success. The band members all came from Melbourne. They'd have school friends and family members turn up. Still, it stung – the change in the kitchen air, the way the others had all looked at each other as if they'd already discussed his absence.

'Simon can drive the truck,' he said. There may have been a hint of derision in his voice – why, after all, did only one of them have a licence? He'd been driving for as long as he could remember: four wheelers, utes, tractors. It wasn't that hard.

'Yeah, but Simon's at his sister's wedding and he's the *usher*.' The accusation lay thick in the air. Being an usher was a real excuse for not turning up to a mate's first gig. Travelling three hours to play a game of footy was not.

He changes gear, listens to the engine make the necessary adjustments, settles into his seat and wonders if they've got that one right. It's a drive he makes every Saturday during the season and each time he wonders why the hell he does it.

He's on the highway now, just out of the city. The sky is orange-pink, a poorly concealed promise, and the kilometres are ticking over – just over two and a half hours to go. Like every week his parents will be at the game today, watching him from behind goal, and afterwards he'll go over to them to hear a quiet and fair assessment. Last year he still brought his washing home for his mother to do but he's stopped that now. Any noble intentions of not taking advantage of her subside, however, when her cooking is involved, and he doesn't say no when she piles up his car with sausage rolls and relish for him and his housemates. He loves those sausage rolls, could do with one right now.

Why does he do it? He slows down to drive through a sleepy town. There's the old coach, of course: tight footy shorts no matter the weather and a whiteboard with movements so calculated they'd rival the desert fox. He demands loyalty. And every quarter-time speech without fail it's the same drill, an old man's plea: 'This game could be it, boys! A new golden age for the club, for the town even! Three quarters to go, boys – believe in yourselves, we can do this.'

No one believes the coach about the game or the town. Just look at the place dying and all the closures.

Just look at the state of the town hall, the numbers in the primary school. Fact is, his hometown is an old dog waiting to be shot and the team won't last another two seasons. There's only so many times you can hyphenate the name of a football club and merge with old rivals.

But no one ever takes the coach to task. He's Super Boot Dowsley, for Christ's sake, saviour of the 1973 grand final, father of two draft nominees and one boy whose white cross he'll drive past just before Derrinallum. The coach is a legend of the town and has been a member of the club for forty-five years. You can't knock him.

He changes gears and slows down, pulling onto the side of the road for a piss. He says hello to the sheep, making out their soft shapes in the half dark, and they bleat softly, just awake. He gets in the car again. Starts up. Passes two towns just waking up and one that never will.

It's not just Super Boot that brings him back to play each week, he thinks as the world rolls on by. It's more than that, though it's hard to work out what the other reasons might be, what with the blue Commodore tailgating him and the signs up ahead telling him to slow down, have a rest, take a break.

Kate Brunt will be at the game today, playing netball in division one. It's soothing to think of her brown arms and strong thighs as she darts along the court. He finds himself doing that in lectures sometimes. Thinking about her and the way she moves. She's Goal Keeper. In Grade Five he scratched their initials on the back of the scoreboard and they're still there for everyone to see.

He thinks of his teammates; blokes he went to primary school with, whom he's been in fights on account of, for and with. They've got names like Carbo and Stitcher and Disco, and they go out with girls in the netball team. He sometimes tells his housemates about these blokes and feels a sting of regret as he does so. In telling his stories, he's feeding into their assumptions about people who choose to live in country towns. He's giving them what they want, making them feel superior about their commerce degrees and pissy houses in the 'burbs. But despite what his housemates think, the boys on his team are not stupid. Half of them have been to uni and returned, smart as anyone he sits in tutorials with, but it doesn't stop them from yelling 'Dazzle 'em with Shakespeare' every time he marks the ball.

The highway must be clogged with young blokes like him. Driving home on Saturday mornings to play for teams with names like Jeparit-Rainbow, Manangatang-Tooleybuc and Tempe-Goya-Patche.

Young blokes on the highway just like him, leaving the city behind. They're all driving hundreds and hundreds of kilometres, full of regret and wonderment at the pull that keeps them returning week after week. At the push that takes them back.

He'll never be a star player, never win the best and fairest. But he's steady, he knows that. He's a strong kick and while he can't turn up to training, he'll be one of the first ones on the ground today warming up. He's barely missed a game in three years.

His team, the Seagulls, gets flogged by ten goals every game, and not a victory in sight. It's making its last squawk, his team, and he'll be there each week to usher in every dying loss in the mud, every slipped mark, every out of bounds on the full.

His elbow is out the window now, and there's a good song on the radio and he's hit the shire boundary. And there it comes, that big ball of a sun, that big ball of orange rising over the horizon. It jolts him every time. Rays light up the stone fences, hit the trees and illuminate the paddocks. The old gums shimmer green and grey in the early-morning light and the world appears quiet and gold. It's like it is every Saturday, a new era.

They might have a chance today.

He's home.

SOLITARY

I reckon I've got two choices. Kill the poor little thing or drop it and run. I'm standing in the bike shed, wall to one side and Fedsy blocking the entrance.

The situation doesn't look good, but then again, not much has since we came here.

About four months ago we moved to the Mallee, from down south where it's cool and green. None of us were happy about it. Still, Dad was fond of saying, with five kids and one on the way you can't afford to be choosy. You go where the work is. Dad, a conservation manager in a town like this! We may as well be lepers.

It was just our luck that we moved here at the same time as the mouse plague began. We hadn't even put our bags down when they arrived, teeming past us into the house like extra family members keen to choose the best room.

They came in biblical proportions, settled anywhere they could and began breeding. They were like some crappy relation at Christmas who never knows when it's time to leave.

We found them everywhere, in the cupboards, in the bathroom, behind the fridge and in the couch. When Mum found droppings in our sheets, she shouted at us for eating biscuits in bed and set traps all around the room.

Even the cats got sick of the mice. Our tabby lay around the house, fat and lethargic like a retired millionaire.

Suddenly, I need to wee. I'm holding on to this meaty moving tail with Kit and Fedsy staring, and it's all I can do to keep it together. I'm going to be like one of those prisoners in war movies who wet themselves before they get shot, leaving the guards laughing and pointing at the stain. I've got to do something. I've never been much good at holding on when it counts.

One night not long ago when the rest of the house was asleep, I had to go to the toilet. Half awake, I lowered my feet to the floor and tried to remember where the traps were. Since we moved here, Dad's been making jokes about people in town trying to get him for his work in conservation, saying that after his talk on the link between the mice and stock feed we might have to go into hiding. I don't know about that; Dad makes a lot of jokes and not all of them are funny. I do know that no one ever takes the pamphlets on soil damage from out the front of his office. I took a whole stack once to try to make him feel better, but then I forgot about them and Mum found them at the bottom of my schoolbag and told him.

Like a cartoon robber, I made my way through the minefield of our hall, inching along the cold walls, listening to the family snore. Scuffling noises escaped from under my brother's door – he'd smuggled toast to bed. Mum would go psycho.

When I reached the laundry, I fumbled around for the light and flicked the switch. The sudden brightness made my eyes screw up like those of a prisoner just out of solitary and I was surprised to discover that our cat was inside.

'Git out!' I said in the pitchy tone I reserve just for him. 'Now!'

The cat turned his head and settled back in the corner of the room. I placed my hand on the sink and leaned sideways to see what he was preoccupied with, hoping that he wasn't hacking up a hair ball; I've got a weak gut.

But I wasn't prepared for the sight. There in the corner of the room, huddled against the wall, was a tiny mouse, shuddering. At first I was confused. What in hell was the cat doing? This was easy prey, yet there he was, paws stretched out, head resting on them like he was watching his favourite show – but then after a moment, I understood.

The cat was *playing* with it. Every time the mouse tried to move the cat would effortlessly slap it back into line. I watched as the little mouse darted this way and that, only to be stopped in its tracks by a fat paw. At one point, the mouse almost made it – it got about two feet away – until the cat leaped easily in front of it, and thud, it was back in its corner again.

A queasy, green feeling came over me. This time the mouse cowered in its spot. The cat smiled – pink jaws opened wide – and rested again, head on its paws. Watching.

'Git out!' I wanted to yell, but as they say, the cat had got my tongue, and my voice came out in a squeak. Instead, I bent down and picked up a gumboot, the only weapon in sight.

Then something truly awful started happening.

The mouse began to try to *jump into the cat's mouth*!

At first, I thought it was attempting some sort of Great Escape, but I was proved wrong. If the cat moved its head slightly the mouse would jump in its direction, determined to reach those pointy white choppers. In a suicidal frenzy it leaped and leaped again, trying to reach the open jaws, exhausting itself in the process. I stood frozen, a scream lodged in the back of my throat. Again the mouse jumped, and again, its whole body shaking with the effort.

The sound of a trap snapping in the background jolted me from my stupor, and I threw the boot hard.

The cat turned around and snarled – a prehistoric warning – before slinking off. The mouse dragged itself away and I scurried back to bed, forgetting all about traps and the toilet.

Meanwhile, here I am with Kit and Fedsy staring at me like I'm their Friday night fish 'n' chips. They're the two most popular kids in Grade Six and I need all the friends I can get.

It's weird – in this place I can find spots near our house where I can lie on the warm red dirt and hear birds and animals scratching and scraping in the low scrub. I can feel how fine the dirt is, like something precious – and it seems to me that if I could understand it, what the soil means, then everything might be okay for Dad and for us.

In this place, I can stand outside our house and watch the wheat paddocks roll on and on, and the sky's so big and I'm all the world and its possibilities. I feel like that a lot here, but then I go to school.

The local kids stick together like glue and joke about the grey uniforms my mother makes us wear, despite there being no dress code at school. They come from big farms and talk about headers, stripping wheat and Massey Fergusons. I can't catch on, no matter how hard I try. The leader of them all is Kit.

She has pink stripes in her hair and green eyes that win every staring competition. Me, I blink all the time – I never win, not once. Dad's always telling us to focus on our surroundings. He says that if we only pay attention to the people in the town and not to where we live, then we'll get stuck. The land is what frees us, he says. Dad says a lot of things and a fat lot of good they do, too.

Just earlier (just earlier!) I was eating lunch with Eddie and the twins on the oval when she sauntered up with Fedsy and a few others. Fedsy is a poor version of Kit, kind of thick, with a laugh like a fox. She looked sideways at Eddie and the twins.

'Geez, there's enough of yez. I can't think what your mum and dad do for fun.'

I concentrated on my cheese sandwich. 'Don't think, Fedsy,' I said. 'It's not what you're good at. Just follow orders like you're used to.'

My words proved to be a small victory and Kit – eyeing the rest of the kids laughing – brushed up against me and whispered, 'Wanna catch mice?'

I nodded (this was my chance!), but she had already slunk away towards the bike sheds where the nests were.

There was a group of kids already there. One boy lit a match and got a small grassfire going at the entrance of the shed, where a small crack in the floorboards lay. It didn't take long. Mice of every size soon poured out, darting this way and that, trying to avoid the boots and planks of wood that bore down on them in an instant. I averted my eyes from the massacre. My sisters and brother had followed and were waiting for me, huddled a short distance away.

There were squelches and shrieks, there was laughing. I tried not to look down.

A mouse ran over my foot. I jumped back.

I looked up to see them all watching me like I was some sort of toy they couldn't work out. A fresh wave of mice came pouring out of the wall and I bent towards them. Scurrying feet scratched at my arm, and using one hand to block its escape, I managed to pick up a small mouse. Its hot little feet moved frantically this way and that, trying to escape. It made me sick, but I took it by the tail and held it between my thumb and forefinger. 'Got it!' I said, shaking and trying to sound pleased.

Kit stood towards the back of the shed, eyeing me with arms folded.

I'm not dumb. I knew what was expected of me from these kids, what was expected from all of us. Swinging my hands in an arc, I hit the mouse against the wall of the shed. There was a rousing cheer. My efforts were only half-assed, though, and the mouse kept wriggling.

'Come on!' the kids cried. 'Finish 'im orf!'

In the background, one of my sisters ran away crying, the grey belt of her dress flying behind her. Taking a deep breath and looking away, I repeated the swinging harder this time so that the mouse thudded dully against the wood. Still it wriggled. God, what did it take?

Desperate, and with blood in my mouth, I bashed it harder, so that for a moment it was still. My stomach churned, my teeth felt furry. Most of the crowd lost interest and left; this was nothing new.

Only Kit and Fedsy were left now, a growing suspicion on their faces.

I reckon I've got two choices. Kill the poor little thing or drop it and run.

If I choose the second option, we're going to be eating lunch on the oval every day till high school. Never mind the big sky and the golden paddocks, my brother will never be asked to play cricket at recess and I'll never get invited to a sleepover.

And so I do it, grinning like Judas and biting my tongue so hard I can taste the blood.

At the very last moment the mouse goes still, as though resigned to its fate. I bash it hard against the wall. There's a squelch, and a dark red stain appears on the wood. Purple guts spill out of its tiny mouth and I drop it to the floor.

I look up to see Kit grinning widely at me, and my heart slows. I feel as though a giant spotlight is trained on me and I can't move at all.

A wet trickle runs down my tights and now I understand.

I'm trapped.

GLORY DAYS

He wakes, heart beating fast and a vision of glory. In his dreams he's flying fast, over low hills, far above the trees and into the stars. He can see lights on the horizon and he's almost there, it's not a moment away, and when he wakes he doesn't mind too much because he's sure he's had a glimpse of what's to come.

Already he can see it: the crowded streets, the smell of perfume and the giant high-rises lit up like lighthouses. It's the prospect of work, of money, of friends and of the night. No more discussions about rain and cows, it will be all about novels and films and culture. Because that's what I can't get here, he thinks:

life experience. He's yearning for it. He's drowning here in a crusty dam, and he must get out.

One more day till he finds out his ATAR score. It's mid-afternoon and he's in his bedroom, legs dangling over the end of a single bed. A blowfly buzzes overhead, making long, slow arcs about the room. He's spent a lot of time in this room since the end of Year Twelve, mainly sleeping and sometimes thinking.

The fly dips near him, then heads across to the window, where it rests a moment on the sill. The term ATAR sounds like something from another planet, and he imagines himself in a brave new world, a hero of sorts, fighting for the common man. His ATAR will determine what planet he'll exist on and he's pretty sure that it will be a good one. Anything under 90 and he'll be gutted. ATAR, he says aloud. Then he makes his voice low and says it in a Darth Vader voice, *ATAR*.

His mother calls him, and he farts loudly in response.

She's at the door in a moment, telling him to get his father because it's time to go to Grandma's.

He grunts in assent.

'Ten minutes, Rob,' she says. 'Get up now, darl.'

His mother doesn't look too bad for forty-seven, but the way she talks, it's like she's a character in some moronic sitcom. He lets out a drawn-out sigh. It's a wonder he came to be born in this family, he thinks, and not for the first time. When, at school interviews, his politics teacher told his parents that his essay on the Russian Revolution was the best he'd ever seen, they stared at him open-mouthed. 'And to think,' his father marvelled, 'he's never been further than Mildura.'

Later that night he'd tried to explain to them about his essay, how he'd argued that the intelligentsia inspired social democracy and bolshevism in Europe. But his parents just kept eating their sausages, laughing at how they must have been a pack of posers to call themselves *intelligentsia*.

Rob gives his shoes a sniff and puts them on. He'll be glad to leave this room. It's too small for him and there's a smell in it he'll be pleased to be rid of.

Outside, the heat smacks him in the face. It's a northerly blast with Wimmera dirt for shrapnel and he covers his face with his hands. The air clings to him and his thighs chafe with every step. A small willy-willy rises out of nowhere and angles its way towards him. He half thinks about racing into the midst of it as he used to do when he was a kid, but it dies down quickly, and all is still again. Well, there goes my excitement for the day, he thinks, and then he says *ATAR* again in his Vader voice.

All about him the land is dying. That's the thing about farms, he thinks, you're constantly reminded of death and never life. Calves drown in troughs, sheep get their limbs caught in barbed wire and die, bloodied and covered in flies. Ewes bleat while fetuses hang out of them and foxes dangle on the fence lines. Even his old man, face wrinkled like a sultana, looks half gone. He finds his dad now, near the shed. He's up to his neck in some sort of animal shit, deliberating.

'Dad!' he shouts over the low din of the animals. 'Grandma's thing.'

His father raises his thumb in understanding, gives his lower back a rub and returns to whatever it is he's doing. All the farmers around here are old, he thinks. It's like some sort of virus hits when people turn eighteen and the young have to leave. He turns back towards the house.

The bird boxes that are supposed to attract rare turquoise parrots are lined up hopefully beneath the sagging gums near the empty dam. No bird has even bothered to shit on them. They're tired sentinels from another era but his mother remains positive. *Once spring comes*, she says every year. She's always on about stuff like that. Always in the garden, planting, mulching, pruning, weeding.

Native grasses and whatnot. His parents are mad for it.

Nature! What good is it? he thinks. Leave that stuff to David Attenborough and all the other old fogies; he's out of here. He goes back inside, returns to his room, lies down and waits.

They arrive at his grandma's to find that there's already a paddock half-filled with cars from the district. When he opens the door to get out, slowly and with great effort, his father gives him a look.

'Wearing strides on a day like this!' he says. 'You'll be hot, Rob.'

This is a conversation they have had before.

'They're not strides,' he reminds his father. 'They're stovepipes.' Stovepipes are like jeans, but they're tight.

Really tight.

'Stick that in your stovepipe and smoke it,' his mother says to his father and they both grin. That grin. He's not a fan. Sometimes it's hard to catch what it means, but not today. He's seen them wink too, though that one is harder to detect. At the parent–teacher interview, for instance, after his father said, 'And to think, he's never been further than Mildura!' there may have been a wink directed at his mother. But maybe not.

His uncle John comes out to the car to greet them.

He's a big man and a confident one for someone who still lives with his mother. John slaps his father on the back, kisses his mother and then turns to him. 'Hot aren't you, mate?'

He scowls. Tries to look cool.

'Rob's wearing stovepipes,' his father says solemnly.

'Too right they're stovepipes,' his uncle says. 'I could cook an egg on you.'

God, how he hates this place. His parents walk inside, and he wanders around the back. His older cousins, the vaunted draft nominees and some of their friends, are already there, kicking the footy around. They're friendly enough in a kind of dismissive way, call him over, ask what he's been up to, but he can tell they don't really care. They're like that with everyone.

He hovers around the sidelines for a while before settling under a grey tree with a packet of chips. The shade is pitiful, but at least it's something.

He looks around. The low hills that surround the yellow paddocks look charred, and the late-afternoon sky is a bleached blue stretched thin with not a cloud in sight.

It could drive a man mad to look at that scene every day.

He thinks about what he learned in Year Eight History and the willingness of Australians from this area to sign up for war. Shit, he thinks, eyeing the parched trees and rusted woolshed – it's no surprise to him. If someone offered him a free trip to Egypt and Turkey, he'd be off in a flash no matter the risk. He eats his chips.

A little girl runs up to him out of nowhere and bats a helium balloon towards him. She's a fat thing with ridiculous hair and her name may or may not be Kayla.

He catches the balloon and bats it back but a gust of wind picks it up and it blows away. It rises fast and high – way above the trees – and begins to travel across the paddocks.

'Sorry,' Rob shrugs. 'You can get another one.'

The girl looks into the sky at the small speck of yellow escaping. Without warning she begins to howl, her mouth a red square of misery.

'You lost my balloon!' she sobs, her fat finger pointing at him. 'You lost my best balloon.' She's really crying.

Her distress stupefies him. He doesn't know what to do. What are little kids *for*?

'Meanie!' the girl shouts, her breath coming in quick hiccups. 'It's gone and I'll never ever get it back!'

There's nothing he can do; she's really cracked it. He wonders at what point he should go and seek help. He considers going to find his mother, when, with relief, he sees a man walking over. The man he soon recognises as a distant cousin bends down to the girl, saying something low and cajoling. She runs away towards the house, her sobs becoming song-like as she darts across the grass and dirt.

The man straightens and looks at him. 'Scaring the kids, are you?'

'I didn't mean . . .'

But the man is unconcerned. He leans his back against the gum tree and lights a smoke, 'They're all a bunch of spoiled brats in my opinion,' the man says, inhaling and exhaling like an elegant dragon. There's a slight accent in his voice. An unfamiliar drawl. Rob asks him where he's from.

'New York. London. Here I suppose.'

The man's shadow reaches out towards him, and Rob feels an odd desire to rest his head on it, to lie on the dried gum leaves and feel the black coolness of the man's shape beneath his head. 'I'm getting out of here as soon as I can,' he tells the shadow. 'I've had it.'

The man gives a strange laugh. 'Well, good luck,' he says. 'It's harder than you think. God knows I've tried often enough, but my best stuff, the stuff the critics all like, is when I write about here.'

'The critics?'

'Plays. I write plays for theatre. Some very good, mostly bad. Not really enough to make a living.'

Rob remembers now – there's a relation, a writer who got away. Rob searches for something to say. 'You must hate it here, hate coming back – after everything you've seen? I mean, it must be so – so boring!' he says more to the shadow than the man.

That low laugh again. 'Oh, I don't know. Maybe.' The man reaches down and picks up a handful of soil, rubs it in his hand. 'This dirt,' he says with a kind of wonder, 'it's all they want me to write about.'

The two of them stare out from beneath their tree.

A dog runs past and a plane flies overhead, its progress slow in the big open sky. The man finishes his cigarette. 'Good luck with the city,' he says, stamping the butt on the ground with his pointy shoe. 'No doubt I'll see you back here for a funeral or something.'

'Don't count on it.'

The man says something Rob doesn't hear and throws him a small rock from the handful of dirt he's been holding. Rob is too slow to catch it and it lands somewhere in the dirt beside him, and by the time he's located it and picked it up, the man has gone. He fits the rock carefully into the back pocket of his stovepipes.

Rob eats the rest of the chips and his mother walks over, her low heels making little dust puffs in the dirt. She tells him to go and see his grandmother before they go.

In a few weeks he won't have to do things like this.

He'll be smoking in some dimly lit bar, watching a girl band or discussing Kafka with friends. He has vague hopes of picking up a girl. Rob follows his mother into the house and thinks about the man he's just met. It's hard to place him. He was like a different species and yet the way he leaned against the tree, the way he sort of moulded into it . . . the image stays in Rob's head.

Inside, there is no air. The blinds are drawn and there's the smell of old skin and something else, more vinegary, that he can't put his finger on. His grandmother is sitting on a chair in the middle of the room, a large television screen blaring in front of her. His mother turns the TV off and the old lady's head whips around towards them surprisingly fast, her throat lagging behind her face, its long flap of skin the colour of chicken.

'Rob's going off to uni this year!' his mother says brightly. 'He's waiting on his ATAR score.'

His grandmother's head falls down onto her chest. She may be sleeping.

'And to think,' his mother says sadly, 'she used to make the best trifle this side of Hamilton.'

His uncle John walks into the room and nods at his sister's words. 'This side of Hamilton,' he agrees. 'Won all the prizes.'

His mother leans closer to the older woman's face and shouts, 'Rob remembers your trifle from when he was younger, don't you, Rob?' His grandmother says something in a bubble of spit, and they all bend in to listen. 'I think she asked if you still like trifle,' his mother says after a pause. 'You should tell her you do.'

'Why? She can't hear a thing.'

'Just do it,' his mother hisses.

He leans into the old lady. 'I still like trifle!' he says to the side of her face. Her yellowed skin is encased in deep, flaky wrinkles and she legit smells of piss.

'I don't think she heard you.' His mother smiles at him encouragingly. 'Say it again.'

He begins to feel something like panic.

'I still like trifle!'

A river of sweat runs down the back of his stovepipes.

Finally, the old lady jolts in her chair. 'No need to shout!' she says through rancid breath. 'I'm not in Sydney!'

'Not in Sydney,' Uncle John repeats, chuckling. 'Classic!'

Overhead, the fan slowly spins.

Later that evening, his mother and father laugh about it.

'Not in Sydney!' his mother says. 'You can't make that stuff up.' She brings out a tray of cold beef sandwiches and a beer for his father, who eats while watching the cricket, boots off and big feet resting on a stool.

For some reason, the tray enrages him. He's so cross he doesn't bother to say thank you when she brings out one for him. She's probably never even heard of, what's her name – Geraldine Greer? – or any of those other historical ladies, he thinks, as he chomps gloomily on his beef and green relish sandwich. But it's probably not all her fault. The only books in the house are by Ken Follett and even though *The Pillars of the Earth* was a pretty good read it wasn't exactly life-changing. Because that's what he's after, a life change. He leaves the crust of his sandwich on his plate and contemplates it angrily.

'I saw that writer today,' he says to his father. 'Your cousin.'

'Eh? Who?'

'Beryl's son,' his mother chimes in. 'Peter. Did you talk to him, Rob?'

He nods.

'Peter? The playwright!' his father says. 'That's a good one. Remember that play we saw of his in the Chaff house, out the back of Denny's?'

'Oh yes!' his mother recalls. 'That was a nice evening.'

'Critics write about him,' Rob says. 'He must be good.'

'Critics!' His father nearly chokes with laughter. 'If you mean Denny's mother writing in to the *Gazette* to mention that the play would have been better off as a musical to give it a *bit of life*, then yes, he's had plenty of critics.'

'Beryl is so happy to have him back for a good while,' his mother says. 'I think he's having a bit of a crisis.'

'He said that he lives in New York and London.'

'And so he does; that is, when he's not fruit-picking in Shepparton or asking his mother for money. Playwright!' His father looks almost cross. 'Next he'll call himself an orchardist consultant.'

Rob finishes his crust, has a drink of water and takes his tray to the kitchen. He walks slowly to his room, passing a mirror in the corridor on the way. His face is a mottled red and his shirt clings to his body. It hurts him to notice that despite the sit-ups he does in his room most nights, there's still a pad of fat in each breast and the kids at school are right, his legs *do* look like wheat silos. His uncle was correct too, the stovepipes are uncomfortably hot, and they don't suit him. They don't suit him at all. In his room, he sits for a while on his bed.

Then with some difficulty he takes off his jeans, folds them and hangs them over a chair. The small rock the man gave him falls out of one of the pockets and lands on the floor. He contemplates it for a second before kicking it under the bed. It hits the steel bedframe and ricochets right back, hitting him somewhere beneath his knee.

When he lies down, he hears the fly again, still buzzing around. It bangs against the window and hovers around the blinds. He gives the wall a slap and it goes quiet.

He stares for a long time into the dark till time seems to stretch and grow thin. Eventually he drifts off to sleep and his last thought before he does is not of the score he will receive the next day or the life he hopes to lead, but rather of the sobbing child, Kayla – her face a plate of unchecked anguish and despair.

FOWLERS BAY

The woman leans on the fridge, counting out her money.

She studies each of the coins up close, looking at the old queen on the back of each one. In the 1980s the Queen looked like a Greek goddess, while the '90s brought her dangly earrings and a higher crown. Pre-Diana and all that. In the latest version, she has a double chin, which is good to see. Realistic. The earrings are back to studs and the perm looks a little tighter. The woman wonders if the coin people had to work out whether or not to add in a turkey neck.

Whatever the case, people will be able to look at that royal face hundreds of years from now. They'll say, wow, I found an ancient coin from 1983.

Thirty bucks left, the woman thinks. May as well treat meself like a queen. She asks for a packet of Benson & Hedges, 25s and a Magnum ice cream. Double choc.

Hands over the cash. A lady with a turtle head stands behind the kiosk. Gives a turtle look.

'You'll need thirty-five for that. Magnum's gone up. Six bucks now.'

'Six bucks!'

'Magnums are the fucken Queen Mary of ice creams. You'd be better off with a Gaytime.'

'Orright,' she says.

'Used to call Gaytimes "poofter clocks", go to jail for that now. You can get a Gaytime with yer thirty.'

'Get that then.'

Turtle fetches the items. 'Enjoy,' she says.

Oh, I'll enjoy. I'll have a gay old time, the woman thinks, putting the smokes in the front pocket of her jeans. She walks outside, feels the sea wind belt her like a whip. Puts the Gaytime behind her back to shield it and finds a bench on the other side of the kiosk, facing the dunes. She wipes a piece of seagull shit off the seat with a leaf and lowers herself down.

As she unwraps the ice cream a big chunk of biscuit falls off the side. Only partly on the dirt – mostly on the concrete. She picks it up and eats it. Five second rule. Leans her head back on the wall of the kiosk and looks at the dunes.

Fucking Fowlers Bay. Who woulda thought?

They rise up in front of her, white sand dunes as big as five houses. Stretching across the coastline for thirty-odd kilometres and, according to the experts, still growing.

Two million years old.

In the heat of the afternoon they shimmer. As a kid, she'd imagined she could see them moving, witness their silent creep towards the town. It scared the shit out of her. She used to jump on her father's knee while he was fishing and beg to leave the place.

Funny, that. Thirty years later and now she *would* have to beg to leave. Got 20 cents change from Turtle after the fags and Gaytime and can't do much with that except buy one of those big gumballs from the machines at the supermarket.

A gust of wind whips up, bringing the dunes with it. Sand everywhere. She holds the Benson & Hedges in front of the Gaytime. Protect it. She'd read somewhere that in Victoria a mother had called her twin boys Benson and Hedges. Poor things. The images on the front of the carton were not cute; you wouldn't want to be reminded of your twin boys when you looked at them. Rotten, bleeding gums; a tongue half ripped out and a grey-looking bloke on a breathing machine.

She lit up a fag. Wouldn't mind a breathing machine right now, she thinks. Can't breathe here in Fowlers Bay with all this fucking sand blowing down my gullet. And yet, here she was. Had chosen to be here. Fowlers Bay, sitting on seagull shit with 20 cents left in her right pocket and the air so big and clean it hurt.

A crunching beside her. Thongs in the golden sand.

Two feet, hairy as all hell in her line of vision.

'You Sandra Correy?'

She looks up. A young bloke who's probably in his twenties stands in front of her. Big bloke, sandy hair, skin flaking off his nose, nodding at her; a friendly nod, not quite a smile.

'Yeah, what of it?'

'Gotcha letter. Got it last Tuesday. Been out trawling, just got in this morning. Came to see you.'

'The letter was for Ron Beamer.'

'Know that. Ron's dead but. Died six months ago. Heart attack on the boat.'

She spends a good while looking at the hairy feet. Her mouth goes dry and she wishes she'd bought a Coke rather than the Gaytime. Cheaper too. Sand blows in her mouth and she spits it out, to the left side of the hairy feet.

Her father had hairy feet. Never without a pair of thongs. When the straps broke, he used to use the plastic tags from bread packets to fix them up. Put them under the thong, under the round bit of the strap. Loved his thongs. Loved every bit of this place, the sand he walked on. The sea his big feet paddled in. He taught her to swim, out here in Fowlers Bay, in between the leaky trawler and the jetty. Forty years ago.

Her mother, Dee, couldn't stand the place. Sand dunes gave her the creeps and she missed the pokies, the loud pubs of Adelaide. After a few years of it, Dee took off, bringing Sandra with her, leaving the old man behind.

Moved to Melbourne. Back to Adelaide and then a stint in Kalgoorlie. Motherhood a trial. Kisses and cuddles one minute then smacks and throwing glasses the next.

Always needing the high life. Dee in Kings Cross now, somewhere. Submitting to the high life.

'You okay?' the young bloke says. 'Don't look too well.'

'I'll be right.' She shifts forward on the seat, puts her head between her knees, takes a couple deep breaths.

'Ron died quick, you know. Started coughing, grabbed his shoulder and fell on the deck. Over in less than five minutes. It's how he woulda wanted it.'

She nods. Feels pain like a shot-put in her guts. No tears. Rubs her legs.

'Take you to the doctor p'raps?'

'No,' she says with some force. 'No more bloody doctors.'

A heaviness on the seat beside her. The young bloke sits down. 'Want me to get someone? Husband, boyfriend maybe? Kid?'

She shakes her head. There's no one. She married the last boyfriend, a whippet of a man named Kane. Kanine, she sometimes called him. Kanine lasted a few years till shit hit the fan, till it all got too hard, the trips up to Perth too expensive. She couldn't blame him for it, he was a nice enough bloke. Deserved someone good, a family, a house.

Never had any kids, although she would've liked to.

There was a woman too, after Kanine. Sal, an ex-nurse with a touch of the martyr. That didn't last long. Sal wanted a noble cause and soon found it in a younger woman. Single mother with breast cancer.

The pink ribbons you can wave about, and the fun runs – Sal would like that.

She takes a few more deep breaths and sits up straight. Takes another fag from the packet.

'Not too good for you,' the young bloke says, 'if you don't mind me sayin'.'

'I don't mind yer sayin'.' She lights up and blows smoke out the side of her mouth. 'You a local?' she asks.

'Yeah, born and bred.'

She recognises the pride. Feels a twinge of jealousy.

'Listen,' he says. 'I read the letter you wrote Ron. Read the part where it says you're his daughter, wanted to come and see him. Go out fishing again and that, like when you were a girl.'

Sudden tears in her eyes. Hot. Ron never got the letter. Dad. She hasn't seen him in over twenty years.

She draws hard on her cigarette and feels a bit of sand on her lips. Jesus. You can't escape those dunes, she thinks, and looking up at them she sees again how enormous, how powerful and slow they are. Idiots drove their motorbikes on them, kids scrambled up and down, but all it took was a soft westerly and all sign of human interaction was erased.

The dunes made time slow. Made the days lengthen and stretch. Fowlers Bay was a place to wait. Her father knew that, with his eye on the weather, on currents and the wind. 'Good things will come for the boats,' he used to say, 'for the fishing line, if you just wait for the right time.'

'Had no right to open my letter,' she says. 'It wasn't addressed to you.'

His hairy foot shoos an ant away from her leg. 'But I open all his mail. I'm Ed Beamer, see. Ron's son, from his second marriage.' He spits some sand to the side and gives her an unsteady smile. 'He talked about you. Got your letters from time to time. Then he heard you got sick, up in Perth. Wanted to come and see you but didn't know where and you changed names that often.'

It was true. First her mother's maiden name, then her stepfather's, now Kanine's.

'I was coming down to see him,' she says to no one, says to the dunes. She *was* coming to see him. Coming to wait with him. All those twenty years she was just on the brink of it. But her mother, her jobs, Kanine and the illness – there was always a reason not to go, and over the years the memory of her father shifted and blurred till all that remained was a faint mirage.

'Dad left you a bit of money, not much. And the old house, the one you grew up in. Bit of a wreck. Got papers for you to sign.'

She nods. Feels a pain down her spine. Rubs her lower back with the packet of fags.

'I go fishing every night. Near the old trawler.' He cocks his head towards the harbour and rubs his hands. Big paws and a thick covering of yellow hair all over his legs and arms. Long eyelashes; the girls, if there were any, would love him.

'You can come if you like – show ya the best spots. Be good. Be good fun, Sandra.'

Hot tears spring unbidden.

'You look like him,' she says, and she can tell he likes it.

'Fishing? Tonight? You want to come?'

'Yeah,' she says. 'I want to come. I would like that very much, Ed.'

He nods, spins around on his thongs and walks away in slow, long steps. She puts down her fag, stubs it out. Folds the Gaytime wrapper and gives a little laugh. A bark. She has a brother, a younger brother, and in a few hours she'll be fishing with him. She looks at the dunes, glowing in the remains of the day. Sand will cover us all in time, her dad used to say, but at least in Fowlers Bay you can watch it come.

A soft breeze blows up. Westerly. She puts her face towards it and breathes in the warm air and gritty particles of sand. Year by year, day by day, minute by minute, she thinks. It's coming for us all and it's a beautiful, annoying, terrifying thing and all we can do in the meantime is live.

COACH

Get in there, Ryan! Back up your teammate. C'mon. Call for it! Call for it! That's it, that's it, nice handball, Hunter, well done – now pass it on, that's right, look to the wing – Logan's on his own! Hey, Logan! Get your hands out of your pockets! Never mind, next time, mate. C'mon, Doggies, I can't hear you, get the talk up, talk, talk, talk! Stay on your feet. Don't go to ground! Up ye get, Alex – up, up – that's it. Now hunt the ball.

What's the score, mate? Eh?

Yeah, we should do quite well this season. Got a couple of gun recruits from St Therese's and what with the two boys from Year Ten we're allowed now, we should do alright.

Hands up, Luca! Hands up!

Last season was a complete mess. Had kids playing who didn't know a handball from a sponge cake. It's the soccer of course, slowly killing our game.

Kick long, Bohdi! Angus, protect the space! Protect the space!

You can't complain, though. As long as the kids're out there playing sport it's okay – that's what I say to the other parents. They're only young – plenty of time to school them in our game.

Hunter – Hunter . . . yes! Great goal! Well done, mate!

That Hunter's a good player. I first saw him kick a ball in kinder and I just knew – he had it, you know? That ability that some people have – that ability to just read the ball. And that speed and grace that just a few are blessed with. It's in the genes, that sort of football talent, it's been passed on from proud father to son and father to son again. It's funny how that works out.

Score, mate?

We should win today. If Hunter keeps his head and passes it on occasionally. I like his drive, I like his competitiveness, but that's not what it's all about in the under fourteens.

C'mon, boys – hunt the ball! Hunt the ball!

He's got to learn to pass it on, to share it with his teammates. See Josh over there? Wing? Hasn't got a kick all game.

What's that, mate?

Oh, I stand corrected, he's had two handballs. Yeah, no kicks yet, but when he does, you'll know about it.

Torpedoes like you've never seen. Imagine when he's in the . . .

Carn, Josh, mate! Get in there!

Well, at least he tries . . . I remember when I was their age. Just the same. Every Saturday morning dressed in my socks and footy boots, jumper tucked in, 'Eye of the Tiger' on the record player – as eager as you like.

Couldn't wait to get out there. Just like these kids.

See Tyson over there? Half-back flank? Lives in a caravan down the river. Single mother, three kids, Tyson the eldest. I pick him up each week; Mum doesn't have a car and he's there in his footy gear, clutching that yellow Auskick bag like it's a golden ticket. He'll do okay. He's got his head screwed on right. As for young William on the wing – now what he needs is some boundaries. I've spoken to him about talking back to the umpires, how it's best just to put your head down and carry on – ahh, but we'll see.

They're good boys. All good boys. Known most of 'em all their lives. Played footy with a lot of their dads – and seen how talent can be hereditary. Hunter there, he's got a run on him just like his dad, and Fraser is the spit of his old man. Funny though, how biology can sometimes trip us up. Ned's dad played for Footscray but his kid can't kick to save himself. In a decade or so these boys'll all grow up and leave this town – for some of them it'll be an escape and for others a wrenching so hard it'll never quite go. Saying goodbye to their school mates, their mums and dads, the same girlfriend they've had since they were fourteen . . . The sound of the cockies, the sharp smell of gum and hot dirt after a rain. This place, this place, it gets to you.

Give him room, Bohdi!

But all of them will remember their footy, you can be sure of that. They'll remember the rindy half-time oranges, the frost on the oval, the goosebumps from cold or nerves and the day they got ten or more possessions.

They'll remember running with the flight of the ball – that wide arc and the quickened breathing, the long, slowing strides and when they finally mark it, ten metres out from goal, it'll be a birth of sorts.

The call of the old bush ovals – I hear it still. I can't drive past a game without slowing down and half wishing I could pull the boots back on – in spite of the crook back, the Achilles, and the shoulder that's never fully healed. Because it never really leaves you, that love for the game.

You see them, of course, blokes in their forties, filling up the seconds – chasing the younger blokes down the ground with the look of the old farm dog that knows he's beat.

Look for your teammate, Tyson!

I had my time, had my fair share of physio appointments and Deep Heat. It's coaching now. These kids and the thirds. I'm here most days for training and for the games on the weekends. On evenings when I'm not at club meetings my wife goes crook when I get the whiteboard out.

She says I'm obsessed. Obsessed? Now that's a funny word.

You right, mate? Need a drink? Hold the cup with two hands, two hands, mate – that's it. Good boy. What's that, mate? No, you need to drink. Drink for Dad.

Obsessed. We first knew there was some sort of problem with Jeremy here when he was about two.

Didn't speak, didn't play with his toys – just liked opening and shutting the drawers on the coffee table.

He'd open and close those bloody things all day if we'd let him.

Talk, talk, more talk, Doggies!

That was hard, the repetitive stuff. But it was the lack of communication that got us. No cuddles, no kisses, no bedtime stories. And no football, of course.

Couldn't stand to be with the other kids on the ground and didn't like the feel of the ball. Hated it. Hated all team sports, especially soccer – which is fair enough.

He's the same age as the players. Born the same week as Hunter.

I see the other parents come to watch their boys play.

Standing in the rain with their arms crossed, trying to keep a lid on their pride. Dads mostly. Looking at their sons and remembering their own time as a boy and the glory days still to come off the field and on it.

Don't know what glory days Jeremy'll have. I'd like him to have a friend over for a play one day.

Run with the ball, Fraser!

Like him to have a kick-to-kick with me, that'd be good. But you know what? In his own way, in that locked-up, private world of his, Jeremy does see the beauty in the game. It's just a beauty in numbers that I don't see so well. He knows the full name, age, weight and number of every player in the team. He knows the scores, can tell you every stat and will replay every game touch by touch whether you ask or not.

Look for your, teammate! Good boy, Ned!

We make a good team on the sidelines, Jeremy and me. Come rain, hail or shine he'll be here beside me, calling the stats. And as the boys in this team grow up and leave, go on to play footy in other cities and towns, my boy will stay with me. Here in this little old town of ours.

Of course, I do wonder what it would've been like to have a son like Hunter or Fraser. And then I look down at my little bloke here, my beautiful boy, and I think – well, I've got about the best son in the world . . .

Call it obsession or love, but we've got it in spades in the coach's box. You could say it runs in the family.

TWITCHER

The barking owl. *Ninox connivens*. Rare but not endangered. Not protected but possibly should be according to some. He'll be looking for a mate. Highly unlikely around here, what with all the noise. End of football season. Hoodlums in cars heading up this way for drinking parties and god knows what else. Disturbing the peace. I cannot wait for it to be over.

I wrote a letter to Parks Victoria about this place, quoted from another letter I'd received from the *Twitchers Tribune*:

> *This environment is unique for birdlife, being warm enough for the rainbow bee-eaters and cool enough*

for the dollarbirds. Surely this is reason enough for the authorities to make this area into a wildlife heritage park; free of cars, motorbikes, dogs, guns, generators, campfires and drinking parties. I have been birdwatching in this area since I was a boy and have long witnessed the devastation wrought upon the native species.

Apart from the football parties at the end of the season, not many people come here. There's a peace in this part of the world that's all too rare now. I like it.

There's no bustling, no pushing, no prying. I do meet other twitchers here occasionally, mostly men. They know just to nod and move on, perhaps discuss any regent honeyeater sightings. Twitchers understand the importance of quiet. Of the wait.

I waited for a letter back from Parks Victoria – received nothing in the mail, nothing at all.

But did get a visit from the police.

Yes, the police. I was surprised. But I've always respected our force and so I fixed myself up as best as I could and came down from the tree I was in.

'You make a habit of that?' the officer said, all surprised when I jumped down beside him.

'Well yes,' I said. 'It's the best way to scout out the natural surroundings.'

'You do a bit of that?' he asked. 'Scouting around?'

Well, I thought that was a peculiar sort of question. How else do you observe birds if not by watching, waiting and scouting around? It's an acquired skill, birdwatching. It takes patience and time. You have to be dedicated. It can take hours, days, weeks, even, to find the perfect bird. I've had to learn to adapt, blend in with my surroundings, take up little space and wait.

He asked me if this area is good for birds and I had to chuckle. Good for birds! Ha! Does a masked booby dive?

Wait! Listen! Thought I heard something.

I saw a couple of spur-winged plover chicks last week. Little things, left all alone in their scrape. Mother must've been killed by foxes.

The policeman asked me about the football trips in the bush, all the shenanigans they got up to and whatnot. I told him all I could, all the details of the drinking games and the huge bonfires and the songs. The policeman laughed and I couldn't help but get the impression that he wished he'd been on one of the trips too.

The policeman asked if I'd ever seen any girls with them.

Oh, I'd seen them. Seen more than I wanted to of them as a matter of fact. Barely sixteen and the things they were getting up to in the bushes with those football yobbos. I told him that I'd seen them. Two young girls.

Dressed like common babblers and shouting like a pair of bush stone-curlews.

The policeman asked me to make the sound.

I made it, it's a chilling sound. Listen! Magnificent.

The policeman wrote something down and went and made a phone call. He asked for my address. I live with my mother, so I gave him her details. He asked me if I ever got lonely being out in the bush all by myself.

I said no. Well, I'm not by myself, I added, I've got the birds and they talk to me.

The little tweets and shrills, I'm beginning to under-stand them – getting to know their movements, their habits. After all these years, I'm beginning to commu-nicate with the birds . . .

The policeman asked me if I'd heard about the missing girls.

There it goes again! That barking owl – it's here somewhere. Always looking for a mate. It will be hard for him, but he's cunning, that owl – he's a predator and he is the master of stealth.

I hadn't heard about the missing girls. Told him I don't bother with the radio and newspapers so much. I read the *Twitchers Tribune*, but that's about it by way of current affairs for me. He said one of them lives near me. The Morrow girl. Freckle faced, like a spotted mink.

There was scratching in the tree house above us and the policeman grabbed at his side, like an American cop in a movie. He asked if he could see my tree house and I said yes and showed him the ladder I'd made.

Up he went. Up, up the policeman climbed – and me right behind.

I could see the bottom of his shoes; there was some African lovegrass stuck to his sock. That shoe would have to be cleaned before he left. Cleaned and scrubbed so that not a speck of the lovegrass could contaminate the land.

Up the policeman went, and me right behind. When he got to the top he held tight to the tree branch and stared at the little box I'd made in the corner. There they were. The two little chicks that were left all by themselves in the bush. Still huddled together and frightened despite all my efforts at communication.

It's high in my tree house. My bird-viewing platform is almost five metres from the ground. But heights don't bother me. At boarding school in the city when I was ten, the bigger boys pushed me onto the roof of the cathedral and closed the hatch. It was cold. And dark. And high. At first, I was afraid. I shouted and shouted and called out, but after a while they forgot about me.

A nun saw me there the next morning and some men had to help get me down. My mother was very cross and the other boys were punished. But that night on the cathedral, I learnt something important – once you forgo your terror, there is no need to be afraid of open spaces, the endless air and the wind. I could transport myself back home just by listening.

'Well,' the policeman was saying, 'look at that. They're just two little birds.'

And while he was going on about investigating all leads, I could already imagine just stepping off the platform and diving into the air – feeling the cool wind beneath my beating arms.

The policeman asks me what sort of bloke I am but . . . listen!

There it is! There it is!

Me?

I can hear it!

I'm just a bloke who likes birds.

OVERCOAT JOE

In the car on the way to the Mallee town where my husband grew up, we don't talk much. We watch as the land becomes wider and flatter and redder and we take turns to drive, leaving the engine and handbrake on as we run around the car to swap seats every couple of hours.

It's Christmas time and we see a few hay-bale Santas in the paddocks we pass; there're red tinsel chains tied to tractors, blowing in the wind. I'm liking the trip, but my husband becomes quieter as the kilometres pile up.

My husband left this town when he finished school and rarely came back. His parents are still there, they just moved into a new place when the family home burnt down, not long after they'd sold. Terry warns me that the new place won't be much, but I don't mind. His parents are friendly people and while we don't see them often, I like talking to them on the phone. Every year his mother comes to the gardening roadshow in Melbourne and we have a good afternoon there together.

I remember to check the contents of the boot in one of our driver swaps. There's salvia and rosemary shrubs I've potted up for Barb's new garden. Tough plants that don't mind the heat – but I'm conscious that five hours in the boot might be a stretch too long, so I spray them with a little water pump thing I've brought from home.

All the way, those big, flat red-brown paddocks bake in the heat. The trees grow shorter, become shrubbier, become yellow grass, and in the last hour there's barely any vegetation at all. From inside the car it looks expansive – you could run for miles and miles, you could dream big in country like this. But outside the heat is stifling and we're forced back into the car when a gust of red dirt smacks us in the face. It's a sharp reminder: wake up, we've left the city! I squint through sandy eyelashes at the vast world beyond. Back in the car, we're lulled again. I fall asleep.

*

After five hours we turn off the highway and my husband points to a block of land to the left. 'See there,' he says. 'That's Overcoat Joe's.'

The place he points to is badly neglected. A weatherboard with a roof caving in and a chimney falling apart. Plants and weeds cover the front path and the trees sink into each other as if they're drowning.

'Location, location, location,' I say.

Terry doesn't respond. He slows down and I see a couple of birdbaths in the front yard, under the trees. There's crabapples, scrubby gums and Mallee shrubs. Two windows are smashed in.

'Overcoat Joe,' Terry muses and we turn into the town.

Terry's parents' house doesn't have a garden. It is full of stones and hot dirt. There's a tree there, but it's dying for lack of water. A northerly springs up and a broken blind bangs against a window.

His parents come out to meet us, faces red and parched. 'Come in, come in!' They urge us to get out of the heat. We stumble into the small lounge room where the air conditioner pumps out freezing air to a rhythmic beat. Photos of Terry and his sister at their deb balls adorn the wall. It's all white and lace and big hair and soft focus.

We stand around the air conditioner and then we sit around it. We talk about the harvest (bad) and wheat prices (slumped). There's a smell of stale water. We drink hot tea and eat corned beef sandwiches. There's grapes, half frozen, in a metal bowl, and fruit cake. The air conditioner chokes for a moment and we all hold our breath before it chugs back into life.

That night, at my request, we go to the pub. There's only so many childhood photos of Terry I can take. I hobble along the asphalt in my new wedges and link my arm in his.

'Having a good time?' I ask.

'I'd like to be on the road by nine,' he says.

The Commercial is pumping. It's one of those old-time pubs, built in the heyday when wheat was king and sons stuck around. We make our way through the front door, feet sticking to a carpet that's seen better days. We bypass the ladies' lounge and move straight to the bar. Terry recognises a tall man leaning on the wall, black and white photos behind him like he's about to give a talk.

'Carbo Wilson!' Terry says and walks over to shake the man's hand. I'm introduced to Carbo Wilson and the two men are soon in discussion about the state of the local oval. I look around the room and drink my beer in quick gulps. The bar is full of men in checked shirts and women drinking vodka cruisers. There's a band starting up, two men and a woman with a country-style twang. A group of men play pool under a framed print of dogs playing pool and an older lady sells me a raffle ticket for a prize I don't want to win. Terry buys Carbo and me another beer.

I feel myself relaxing. A glass smashes somewhere in the pub and someone yells, 'Taxi!' Pubs are the same everywhere, I think fondly. I like pubs. A pub is where I met Terry. My husband is still talking about the 1990 AFL Grand Final, where his town beat the slightly bigger town in what the other man claims was an epic match. Ten goals down at half-time and their ruckman, Oysters Dean, was off with a hammy. I zone out and drift to the bar, where someone else tells me about the 1990 AFL Grand Final. I say, 'How's about that comeback?' and they beam.

After a few drinks I meet Oysters Dean and I fall upon him like he's a hero. 'How's your hammy!' I yell and he's handsome as you like. His hammy is better but now he's got a crook shoulder from where he fell off the four-wheeler. I get another beer and look around for my husband. He's still there at the doorway, talking to a different man – bending down and nodding.

I wave to him to come over, but he signals to me that he's talking and I nod. Terry's not exactly your most outgoing guy. Someone asks me who I am and where I'm from and soon I'm telling a story to a small crowd, because if there's one thing I know how to do well, it's tell a tale. Soon they're laughing about the time I bowled Terry out for a duck at the office Christmas party and how he got the office dress-up day mixed up last year and came to work in a toga.

I meet another farmer named Sven who lived in Ireland for a year. His real name is Steve. Sven was too old to play in that 1990 game and, instant allies, we stagger to the DJ to request Springsteen's 'Glory Days'.

The band does a semi-passable rendition of the song and Sven and I dance and sing along. Afterwards, I meet someone named Jake, who is good-looking in a kind of cocky, boy-band way.

'Terry's done well for himself,' Jake says to me.

'*I've* done well for myself,' I say. But I know what he says is true.

Jake takes a long swig of beer and steps a little closer. 'That right?'

'Yep.' I take a step back.

'Terry ever tell you about the egg war?' he asks.

'The egg war? No, never heard of it.'

'It was epic, every kid in town was involved. Terry would remember it.'

'Would he now,' I say, and I yell, 'Terry! Come over here.'

But Terry's deep in conversation with the same old man and doesn't look around. I lean in close to Jake and he says, 'What we'd do, see, is get heaps of eggs from the chooks and go around pelting them like mad all around town and at each other. We had a van we'd stay in and then at the last moment we'd open the door and pelt them as hard as we could.'

'Oh,' I say, 'I bet Terry would have loved that,' although I'm not too sure.

'Well,' Jake says with a sideways smile, 'I don't know about that. It was Terry we were egging, see. A few times he'd duck into the house and we'd throw them right after him. We figured his parents probably wouldn't even notice a thing.' The music stops and I curl my lips into a thin smile.

'That wasn't very nice,' I say.

'Aww, we were only kids.'

'Arsehole kids.'

He's not smiling anymore and he looks over the top of my head and around the bar. 'Yeah, well,' he says.

'Stuck up fucking moles like you wouldn't understand what fun was if it smacked you in the arse.'

He walks off and I want to say something clever but I can't think of anything. I just stand there like a village idiot. Jake saunters over to a group of men and they begin laughing. Oysters Dean pretends to throw something my way and, to my shame, I flinch. More laughter. I feel the beer churn and I want to get out of here. The band starts up again and a drunken couple stumble into me, pushing me to one side. I spin around, looking for Terry, but he's gone and I make my way to the door, arms in front like I'm blindfolded. Sven's face appears, pink and doughy. I push past him. People part to make way for me, figures blur. The doors of the Commercial burst open.

Outside, the stars fall and the sky leans low. It's as if someone has engineered the whole sky to droop just as I walk out. I lean over my knees and breathe deeply for one, two, three, four, then I straighten and gaze again into the starry night.

I'm a couple of minutes into my walk home when I hear a low 'hey' and I make out Terry's figure standing underneath a tree. He says he's been waiting for me and wants to show me something.

'I'm never drinking again,' I say.

'Really?'

'I might spew.'

Terry waits while I rest my head on the trunk of his tree. Bright stars wobble.

'And plus,' I add. 'I hate your friends.'

'They're not my friends.'

'They're mean.'

'Yeah. I've told you that.' It's true, he has.

Part of me wants him to go back into the pub and challenge Jake to a duel, but it's quiet here and the faint warm breeze makes this starry night a thing of beauty. I'm grateful for Terry's cool hand and sober voice as he leads me across a dusty park and over a low fence. We're in the scrub now, small bushes and warm dirt. I am led up a small incline and when we reach the top, the Mallee and the small town spread out before us. There's only a faint moon, but I can make out the pub, the pool and the shop. Houses are dark squares. There're no lights on where Terry's house must be.

Terry points out an old building at the bottom of the hill on the opposite side of town. I can see an old shed, falling down, with stumpy trees all about it. I ask what it is.

'It's just a shed, part of Overcoat Joe's land. You can see it all from here, look beyond it.'

Stretching out in a rectangle kilometres long, the darkness behind the shed is more dense and compact. It takes me a moment to realise that it's vegetation. All around it, as far as the eye can see, is sparse land, mown paddocks, cropped and spare, but Overcoat Joe's land is thick with trees, shrubs and grasses. It's as if the whole of the Mallee has crammed into this rectangle and thrived. I ask him if Overcoat Joe still lives in that house we saw.

'He died a year ago – that was his brother I was talking to at the pub.' Terry pauses and then begins talking again. I sit down and filter fine sand through my fingers.

I listen.

'Joe was known as the town weirdo – kept his yard a shamble, didn't tidy up the scrub, had weird ideas about farming and the land, et cetera, et cetera. Truth is, he was probably pretty smart. He was pasture cropping years before it was fashionable – never touched pesticides or used big-time machinery. Grasses waist high. Animals all together in the one paddock, lambs staying with their mothers for months. Knew the names of the plants, knew the stories of this area, all the really old ones. Read a lot. Never married, never had children. Just kept to himself, him and his animals on this farm.

That overcoat – he wore it every day, all day. That didn't help with the teasing. His brother told me that when they found him dead in his paddocks he was wearing it. Turns out it was made of Gore-Tex. Probably the best type of outfit for this climate.' Terry spreads his arms expansively over and above the dark rectangle. 'People were cruel here – graffiti on Joe's shed, smashed windows, called him names. After a little boy went missing one afternoon, you can just imagine what people thought. Turns out the kid was at his friend's house eating ice cream, but it didn't matter. The accusations stuck. Adults, kids, the whole community – people stayed away from him.'

Terry points to the old shed visible down the hill.

'That's where Overcoat Joe kept his pigeons. He bred them, let them fly about everywhere, fed them and so on. I used to come here sometimes after school and watch him train them. Once I asked him if I could have one and he said yes, but only if I didn't keep it in a cage. He gave me a baby one and I named it Peter.'

'Sorry, but kind of a crap name for a bird.'

'Yeah, well, Peter escaped a few days after I got him home. Probably went back to Joe's.'

We sit in the quiet night, breathing in the warm air and feeling the dirt beneath us. After a while Terry helps me up and we walk home slowly, arms linked, feeling the night's caress. The houses in the town are shut up and silent and the streets are wide and bare. I take my shoes off and Terry piggybacks me over the stony front yard of his parents' house.

In the morning I'll have a hangover and the air conditioning won't help. We'll leave after breakfast and on the drive home I'll look out the window at the shorn paddocks rolling by and I'll think of Overcoat Joe and all the nature crammed into his block like it had fled there. I'll think about that pigeon, flying away from Terry's house, above the town and towards a place that recognised the odd, the injured and the introduced.

I imagine the man in the dark coat, eyes to the sky, watching the bird return to his land.

It'll be hot outside when we stop for a break, but I'll wrap my cardigan around me and for a long time I'll stand there, remembering Overcoat Joe.

DESOLATE

It's one of those days that almost kills you, it's that beautiful. Blue, blue sky and a sun so sharp it hurts to open your eyes wider than a slit. The sand is hot and rough, biting into your toes so you have to put your thongs back on till you reach the shallows, and then the water is so cold you gasp. It's always like this. The 90-mile beach is wild. Unlike the romantic coves and family-friendly bays beloved by most Australians, this beach is unpredictable. It is not a swimming beach, with its notoriously treacherous rips, and the constant choppy waves mean that surfers never grace its shores.

You've got 45 minutes till you have to pick up the kids from childcare and this walk is freedom before the hell of evening begins. You walk purposefully in long, confident strides.

There's not one cloud to blemish the boundless sky and, beneath it, the Tasman Sea surges, gathering strength before relentlessly pounding the yellow shore. This area is known for its desolation. The real-estate agents and rich baby boomers haven't cottoned on to the gem that is this part of Victoria, and for the moment you're glad of it. A year ago, you moved here from the inner city to a small farm on the outskirts of town. You and your husband agreed that St Kilda was no place to bring up kids. Its barely disguised air of yuppiedom did little to hide the threat of violence that lurked beneath. Aging backpackers eyed you up and down on your way to get milk. On weekends, carloads of males hurled abuse at prostitutes, sometimes throwing eggs, which occasionally ended up in your yard. A syringe disposal unit in the playground toilets did nothing to quell your fears about the druggies that wandered around ghost-like seeking new ways to end their misery. Mothers in the area told harrowing tales of paedophiles in Luna Park and homeless youths on ice. Your car was stolen twice.

You're glad, so glad you moved. A few goats, new llamas, a chook shed and your family. You've never felt so happy. And there's the ocean, of course. You walk up to your knees in the freezing water, look out to the horizon. On some days you can see the outline of an oil rig, but not today. A school of fish leaps out in front of you and you cry in delight before thinking that maybe they're being chased by something bigger. By a dolphin!

Or a shark, you think.

Great whites have been caught here; you've even found a shark's tooth on the beach. You hop quick-smart out of the shallows and back up the shore.

Continue your walk.

Far off in the distance a gull struggles against the wind, beating its wings in vain against the onslaught of the offshore gale.

Desolate. The word springs to your mind again.

Isolated, uninhabited, uncivilised.

Your stride falters a little and you curse before regaining your step. You know what's happening.

Shut up! You tell your mind. Shut up and let me enjoy this walk!

But now it's happened. From somewhere in the grey recesses of your brain, a latch on a window has just been released. It was almost inevitable. And through the tiny gap, a sliver of fear creeps into your mind. Despite yourself, you look around, up to the sand dunes, covered in spiky grass, and the mass of tea-trees behind. It's the same as far as you can see, and it's a long way to the road.

You keep on walking, but now it's more of a trudge and you look behind you a couple of times before stopping completely.

The window in your mind opens slightly further, and a fresh gust of alarm rushes in. Was that a fin out there, cutting through the shallows? Was that a face, there among the dunes?

Senses ringing, you turn around and begin the trek back home. What's the use in continuing? The walk is ruined. Ruined! Why does this always happen?

Why can't you just relax and enjoy the moment? This beautiful scenery that holds no malice towards you at all. This paradise, this place you've always dreamed of.

Angry, you march along the beach towards the car park that now seems so very far away.

All the thoughts you tried to hold at bay come flooding in.

Three children stolen from a beach, a schoolgirl raped on her way home from school. Serial killers, muggers, perverts and tortured backpackers. Even this place is not entirely free of crime! Three years ago a young girl was randomly bashed and left to die on this very beach. The attacker was found and locked up, but it just goes to show.

You think about all those Reclaim the Night marches you went on, and the fat lot of good they did. You remember striding along with a multitude of other women singing Tracy Chapman songs, and the distinct smell of sandalwood. How you laughed in the faces of those men who jeered at you! How a thousand women can be so brave and united against the bigots, the misogynists and the rednecks of Melbourne.

But there's not a thousand of you now.

There's just you.

Just one.

On this beautiful beach.

This desolate, desolate beach.

Now you're striding and you snort when you remember being ten years old and that the thing you were most scared of was quicksand.

Russians too. Quicksand and Russians, that was what kids were scared of in the '70s. If you were a Catholic girl, include the fear of getting word from God that you were destined to be a nun. Now that was some scary shit.

Hang on, was that something? Something in the . . .

You slow down, because suddenly there's a black dot in the distance.

Someone is coming.

The black smudge grows and now you can clearly see the figure of someone running towards you. It's not a smooth run, their arms are all askew, their body alternatingly bending and straightening like a puppet being put through its paces.

You stop completely, unsure of what to do.

Unease turns fast to panic.

Do you run to the dunes? Into the water? But it's cold and dangerous; you'd be swept away in an instant.

What to do? For a second you spot the silhouette of an oil rig on the horizon.

And all too quickly, she's here.

Wild, wild hair and eyes glazed with terror.

Her screams reach you before she does, and after a moment of hesitation you spring into action – running towards her and grabbing her by the hand.

'Help!' she sobs. 'He tried to attack me! Rape me! Help me!'

Her cries are rambled, jumbled things, but she's in your arms and for a brief moment you hold her, smoothing her hair and listening to her heavy, uneven breaths.

Your terror is at full volume now, you can barely speak, but it doesn't take a brain surgeon to realise that a second dot in the distance, the menacing stick figure headed this way, is the one she's fleeing from – and you pull her, blithering mess that she is, up the beach and into the dunes.

Somehow you get her to be quiet.

You point to where the man is coming along the beach and signal to her to be silent. Her face is mashed into the sand, sobbing silently, and she's grabbing bits of spiky grass, though it must hurt like hell.

It's like a dream, this situation: the worst fucking nightmare you've ever had and you can't believe a moment ago you were thinking about quicksand.

Taking a chance, you raise your head ever so slightly above the grasses to see the man below.

He's there alright. Walking along the beach in careful strides, looking about him all the while. For a second you worry about footsteps, but then you remember that there are prints all over the beach, from the fishermen, the other walkers and the joggers. He knows roughly which direction you're in, though, and as you put your head down quickly, he speaks.

'Come out! I know you're out here somewhere! Come out!'

The girl beside you has gone completely still, and it's hard to know whether she's breathing at all.

'Come out!' he implores. 'I don't want to hurt you! What happened? I was just being friendly.'

Silence. And then his voice sounds again, a little further off this time. 'Look, I'm going now. I don't need this, I'm going.'

You peep your head up once more. He *is* leaving; his steps have quickened now and he fast becomes a black jumble of lines again. All is quiet.

You can barely believe what just happened.

'He's gone,' you say to the still figure beside you. 'It's okay.'

She sits up and wipes at her face with the sleeve of her shirt. 'Thank you,' she says through tears. 'I thought he was going to rape me.'

'He's gone.' Your breath is fast. 'It's going to be okay.'

There's silence while you scratch your head and look up and down the beach once more. It's clear again, empty of everything but the lone gull skirting the shallows.

'I got a good look at him,' you say. 'I don't think he was from around here.'

'No,' she says softly, 'he's not from around here.'

'But you are?'

'I used to be.' She sniffs.

The wind shrieks through the dunes and you look out at the ocean. You know from an old surfer boyfriend that the most dangerous rips lie underneath the smoothest parts. That glassy stillness is a perfect camouflage for the turmoil and strength beneath.

'What happened?' you ask.

'I thought he was nice.' Her voice shakes. 'I met him on the beach and we were having a nice talk, but then he started acting weird and asking if anyone knew I was there. He pulled me down – tried to . . .'

'It's okay,' you say. 'I'll drive you to the police station. I wish I had my phone!'

'There's no reception here,' she says.

You let her catch her breath, you give her time.

'He tried to rape me!' She's sobbing quietly, hands covering her face. 'I'm so pleased I found you! I knew you were here somewhere; I saw you at the carpark. I've seen you in town too, at the supermarket and the petrol station. You live at the Honeysuckles, right?'

She's rambling. You nod, patting her on the shoulder, noting her dishevelled top, her bare feet.

'There's no telling what some people are capable of,' she says in a sad voice, a red eye peeping out from between her fingers. 'I guess something *just snapped* in him.'

'Hey, don't make excuses for him – it won't matter to the police if he just snapped.'

'I s'pose not, but he seemed like such a nice person. They always do, I guess.' She sobs again behind her hands.

'The bastard!' you spit. 'I hope they catch him and lock him up for good!'

She rubs her eyes and looks out to the water, and up and down the beach. 'They won't lock him up,' she says. 'Criminals rarely get the maximum penalty nowadays. With parole, you can be out in as little as five years for aggravated assault.'

Her eyes are uneven. One of them looks as though it's scouting for passers-by, and the other focuses entirely on you. She scratches her arm. She's got big hands. Big shoulders and legs.

Desolate. The word pops unbidden into your head.

She continues, 'You get less time if you do the right thing, keep your head down, don't antagonise the screws.'

'The screws?' And now you're thinking – *on my walk I didn't pass one person and not one person passed me.*

'Prison guards, wardens – you know.' She places her hand on your arm.

I don't know, you think. I don't want to know.

'Of course, you get even less time if you're a woman.'

Something somewhere in your brain crashes and the sound is so loud it threatens to drown out the scream you know is coming. You are sinking and there's no one to pull you out. And the sky, the wind, the dunes and the sea have never been more beautiful than they are right now.

'I got three,' she says.

RUSTIK

A café is opening up in town. Impossible not to feel a stab of hope for the new owners, raise a thin cheer for the brave. I saw them earlier, when I was driving back from the bank, and I slowed right down. A young couple cleaning the big windows out the front. There was something in the way they wiped those windows, putting their whole heart and soul into it; it just got me. I usually just slop some newspaper around the glass. But these two – they were really into it! The woman flicked some water on the man and he grinned at her, giving her a little nudge with his hips. It was like some TV show, there should have been a jingle to go with it, but even after what I'd just learned about my finances, it did cheer me a little. I slowed down even more to read the sign. *Rustik*.

I was plunged into gloom again.

Still, I hoped the Rustik would do better than the last new café; that one lasted just under five months. There were many times when I was the only one in it, drinking its terrible coffee and choking on stale banana bread. That one was named Country Style. The owners came up from Melbourne and built it from scratch; they had high hopes of the tourist industry picking up and real-estate prices rising. It had wooden tables inside with checked cotton tablecloths, little glass jars with plants growing in them, the whole place white and spare. It was hard to drive past Country Style and see the owners looking out the window, willing people to come in, faces pale and elongated behind the glass. But this Rustik couple, maybe they were in with a chance!

When I was growing up in this town there was a really great bakery. It didn't call itself a café, but it served coffee all the same. An elderly German couple, Horst and Marlena, owned it and the tourists went wild for their cakes and dark breads. I try not to think about them much and when I do it's mainly because of the coffee. When I left to go overseas, Marlena gave me her sister's address so I could go and stay with her when I was in Berlin. I didn't end up contacting her but now I wish I had.

At the one T-intersection in town, a four-wheel drive towing a caravan was blocking the road. I drove up behind it and waited. The back of the caravan had a map on it, with markings to indicate where the people had holidayed. They must have been around Australia at least a dozen times; the map was overtaken with texta trails. There was a sticker with an Australian flag on the back window that read, *If You Don't Love It, Leave!*

It was hot in the car and I considered beeping the horn. It's not good to be in a hot car. But the door of the four-wheel drive opened and a bloke in his sixties jumped out, one thong after the other and two skinny legs like mottled salamis. He left the engine running, pulled his shirt over his gut and into his shorts and walked over to me, legs apart like a penguin.

'Hey, love,' he said, leaning into my window. 'Which way's it to the burnt parts?'

'You're in them,' I said.

'Really?' His orange face registered surprise. 'Wouldn't know it.'

'There's been a bit of regrowth.'

'Too right there has,' he said. 'We came all the way from Lilydale to see it.'

'Sorry,' I said. 'As you can see, nature's taken its course.'

'Not to worry,' he said. 'We've still got Kinglake to get to, might be more to see there.'

'You can only hope,' I answered.

The man was an idiot. Look closer and you could see that the area had been burnt all over, burnt to smithereens. The new saplings, the blackened trunks, the limbs like ghost arms reaching towards the road.

There were ferns, new bushes and shrubs I couldn't identify, but the tragedy of the ash played out everywhere like a Shakespearean script.

The orange man waddled back to his four-wheel drive and hoisted himself into the driver's seat. If you don't love it, leave, I thought.

When I got home, Anders was sitting in the middle of the room eating an icy pole, watching a show about polar bears. There was a skinny infant bear teetering on a block of ice and Anders said it would most likely drown. I said that the people filming it could probably save it somehow, guide it towards land perhaps – but Anders said the people filming couldn't save it because that would be meddling with nature. They had to let it take its course, he said. The whole crew would have signed some form on not interfering, there would have been certain conditions to the filming and so on.

I had been with Anders for nearly a year and I was beginning to see that we probably weren't meant to be together. His European manner now just seemed rude rather than refreshingly honest and I wanted him to rack off back to Denmark. I told him about Rustik.

'I give them six months,' he said. I thought about the window cleaning.

'I wouldn't be so sure,' I said. 'They looked like stayers.'

'No doubt there'll be a menu with babycinos and arancini balls going up soon,' he said, his feet resting on a box with *Pots and Pans* written on it. 'They'll have a Facebook page too,' he continued. 'Give it four weeks and they'll be serving chips and potato cakes.'

I grew quiet. Anders had been out of work for three months. 'At least they're doing *something*,' I said. Anders kept watching the show.

When I first met him in London, Anders was like this bright spark in the gloom. Someone invited him to a party at our share house in Cricklewood and he stood out among all the Australian men, not just for his shock of blond hair. For a start he danced; this was something rare among the men I hung out with. Anders danced.

He wore things my friends never would – pink shirts and yellow shoes, tight jeans with silver sneakers – and took longer than I did to get ready.

On our first time out, just the two of us, we went to the Tate Modern and drank swanky cocktails. This impressed at a time when I was more accustomed to snakebite pints and kebabs at 3 am. Anders had travelled through Asia, Africa, the Middle East. He told me about his three months in an Indian commune where speaking was only allowed for an hour a day and how he'd smoked a lot of weed in Bhutan, where he'd considered becoming a Buddhist. He was four years younger than me and didn't care a whit. Someone like Anders could have invoked ridicule among the men I knew, but he didn't. He got along as easily with them as he did with women. It was as if he'd always been among us, and we could hardly remember a time when he wasn't there.

Just weeks after meeting Anders, I broke up with my older brown-haired boyfriend, whom I'd been with for years. 'Things have changed,' I said, looking at the sluggish Thames. 'It's time to move on.' My brown-haired boy played with a loose button on his coat and stared at his feet. 'I can't pin you down,' he said and when I said, 'Well, stop trying,' he said, 'Maybe I will,' and at the time I was glad.

When I asked Anders to come home with me and help renovate the business, he didn't hesitate. There was loads of work given all the clean-up and people were apparently making good money out of it. Anyway, he said yes – I suppose it appealed to his adventurous streak. Now he finished his icy pole and snapped the stick in half. 'The students have been here again,' he said, face glued to the screen. 'They want to see you about something.'

I stood next to the fan for a moment, felt the air cool my thoughts. I pulled my boots on, found a hat and rolled open the back door of the shed. The heat smacked me, made me unsteady. I burn easily. As a kid, I'd swim in the creek on hot days – spend hours by myself lying in the shallows, resting my head on some rock, looking up at the canopy of leaves and the blue beyond. Hard now to recall if there were ever these endless forty-plus, cloudless days that choked all effort at play. I wiped my forehead with my t-shirt and retied my hair. Somewhere up high a magpie gave a mournful cry; it may well have come from the bush itself. The heat shrivelled all living things and the birds didn't sing as much or as often as they used to. I started to walk down the bush path to the cottage. Madness to ever come back, I thought and not for the first time.

Madness to ever come back to a place you lived in as a child and think that things could be the same. As a kid this place was *Dot and the Kangaroo* country, deep and wild with thrones of moss to sit on and shiny rocks to build dams with. When was the last time I'd heard the family of fairy possums? I wondered. It had been a while.

But here I am, against the advice of my parents who wisely now live in a newly built home in Yarra Glen, road access in two directions and insured to the hilt. Here I am, trying to recreate my childhood, rebuild the guest houses, get the sheep going again. I thought about the word 'folly', but it felt too English. 'Fucking lunatic' was what my brother said, and he was probably right.

It was memories of the moss throne that brought me back. The moss throne, remnant of a fallen ash, had me spellbound as a child. In that way I was no different to all the other Australians living overseas who return.

We return for the imagined past, for Big M days on the beach, the broad spaces and freedom under an unpolluted sky. We are always in a state of return, but to what we don't exactly know, we can't even explain what we left.

That ancient throne, green with moss and damp with the smell of rich undergrowth, that was what

I held on to. Queen Guinevere would have been so lucky to sit upon such a chair. I'd play around it and on it for hours and once velvet evening settled over the bush, I'd feel a witchy awareness of my surroundings. My eleven-year-old self could hear the final laugh of the kookaburra and the beginning of the boobook owl's sonorous call.

Once I saw a lyrebird step out among the undergrowth, its black and brown feathers an intricate gown. Sometimes the neighbours' kids would join me, but mostly it was just me. When darkness fell across the valley I'd run, half in terror, through the bush to my home.

But there's no moss now and the throne is a splintered black stump, home to bugs and spider webs.

I tapped at the windowpane of the little cottage where the four students were staying, researchers from the university. Neat and polite, they keep to themselves most of the time, wandering about the place during the day and trying to keep cool in the stone cottage in the evenings. Anders and I agreed that they were much more mature than we were at their age. Why weren't they out drinking every night and laughing hysterically with their friends? Once I asked that and they nodded. 'It's because there is so much at stake now,' one answered. Normally I would laugh at a response like that, but the way the young researcher said it stopped my smirk.

The students poured out of the cottage, smiling and nodding. The last one to come out, a young Japanese girl, took me by the hand and began leading me further down the track, into the bush. 'Come with us,' she said in her clipped accent. 'We have something to show you.'

The students were studying the local vegetation and fire practices in the region. Anders and I went with them to a talk about Aboriginal fire management and it sounded like more than good sense to me. I wished everyone had listened to it a year ago. Now the students were focused on trees in the valley.

We passed the vacant block next door. For the most part I kept my eyes down, but I was glad to note that the mangled swing set had finally been taken away. The students didn't speak. A hush came over them and they hurried past.

I was led down the path and into the bush. 'I spent most of my childhood here,' I told them and they nodded politely without turning around. They probably thought I was ancient; I do look older than my twenty-nine years; it's all that sun damage and coconut oil as a teenager. 'But I went overseas after university and I've only been back ten months.'

The Japanese girl turned around. 'It must have changed a lot,' she said, and I nodded. Yes, yes it has.

At the bank this morning, the manager told me they couldn't lend me all the money required to rebuild the cottages. I'd already reached my limit. And now with all the new requirements to build fireproof homes, she said, well, perhaps it was time to look at other options.

It was dark and cool as we walked deeper into the bush, but the old creek had long dried up and I missed the sound of rushing water. I stumbled on a rock and tripped. In front of me, the students walked on in sturdy boots. In some parts of the valley, the fire had jumped over the lower reaches and left whole areas unscathed. This was one of them, and yet it didn't feel as dark or as quiet as it had once been. The sun speared down in sharp lines, dry twigs crackled underfoot.

Two weeks ago, I thought I might be pregnant.

It surprised me, the excitement I felt despite my misgivings about Anders. If I had a child it could play in the bush like I did, be a little bush kid. Turned out it was a false alarm. I didn't mind too much, but still it got me thinking. One of my friends had a baby girl and when I first saw her in her little crib, something in me shifted. The deep cranking of internal cogs when a train track changes course – an altered journey, the need to reset destinations. A false alarm, but still.

The students and I continued down, deeper into the valley. Here it was quiet and dark. Most of the ash trees had not been touched at all. Those majestic beings, it gladdened me to see them. The students were calling and the Japanese girl beckoned me over.

'Acacia,' she said in a low voice, as if the plants could hear and be offended, 'this far down in the valley. We've found it – the sign.'

And they were going on and on about the sign and they were taking photos of the small bright trees, measuring their distance from the nearest ash and cupping out samples of soil from the ground. They were talking about the first sighting of acacias growing in mass this far down in the valley and how they were the ones to find them. There was talk of journal articles and a large grant. They were most excited about a tiny acacia, bright like an exclamation mark right in the depths of the valley, perfectly formed.

I leaned with folded arms against the trunk of an ash and watched them.

The little yellow clump was photographed and measured. The young students stamped their boots, drank from their bottles and talked about methodology.

They wrote things in little notepads and already I could see them back at university, giving lectures on the valley to polite applause. They knew more about my home than I did. As if it was paying respect to their academic prowess, the bush was quiet.

A few days before, I'd commented to Anders that I used to hear birds all the time when I was growing up.

'I can hear them,' he'd said.

'Not my birds.'

'None of them are your birds.' He picked up his phone and started texting his new friends and my old ones. 'They never were.' When I complained about the weather, he'd say things like, 'Why should the weather be considerate of you? It's hot, get over it.' His pragmatism made me long for a snakebite pint.

Anders was making plans for the place. Guest cabins again, yes, but this time solar powered as well as fire resistant. Fewer sheep in the paddock near the house block, and olive trees in the orchard. Anders knew someone with a press and thought that perhaps he could check it out.

After a while the students began walking again, up the valley towards home. Before I joined them, I leaned down to look closely at the revered plant. In the dark grey of the undergrowth, the burst of yellow reminded me of a beautiful and unwelcome wedding guest. All was still. I ran my hands over an old ash and felt a great wave of sorrow. Up above the sun bore down, but here in the valley the trees sheltered me. I rubbed a gum leaf and held it to my nose, I put it in my mouth and clicked my tongue over it.

On the way back, I could hear people out the front of the vacant property next to mine. More rubbernecks on their weekend drive. 'How sad!' the woman was repeating over and over, the click of her phone camera whirring at every pause. 'Tragic!' she said, her eyes never leaving the scene. 'Nine people in here!' the man was saying loudly, looking around for an audience. 'Nine people they found all huddled up in the bathroom. All locals. Just goes to show.'

The students hurried into their stone cottage and I stumbled past the tourists to my place. What was I doing here? I thought once more. Trying to recreate some idea of childhood? But who would want to be queen of such a kingdom? Whole families, forests and animals have perished here. Leave this place to the students, to Anders, to Rustik and the bank.

There was a word I needed then, like a howl waiting in the wings – there was a word I needed, and I couldn't find it. From my bag I pulled out the tiny acacia shrub that I had ripped from the valley floor. I bent towards the fuzzy yellow foliage and buried my nose in it.

It filled my nostrils, got in my eyes and made me blink.

What was that word? The one to describe the tipping point of nature, when the old order is over-taken. It hurts, this word, it's a long-overdue argument, and trying to find it is a bit like peering over the edge of something sharp and slippery and cold.

Anders called out from inside the shed, 'Hey, want to go to a barbie at Rachel and Mick's? They're the ones with the olive press. I said we'd help them with replant-ing. Few drinks near the old creek?'

I closed my eyes and felt a hundred years old. Already he was sounding more Australian than me.

'What happened to the baby polar bear?' I called back.

'What?'

'What happened to the bear? On the show?'

'Oh that. Dead of course.'

I look across the yard at the beginning of the dry valley and the vacant block. The lone magpie sends out another of its mournful cries. But now I've remembered the word. I look down at the acacia's yellow flowers, bright and resilient against the hot dirt. The young scientists had the word – they said it over and over again and now I've got it. *Threshold* was the word I was after.

Threshold.

THE PRECIPICE

Anna was reading her daughter a story when her husband arrived home with some news. A body had been found at the bottom of the Precipice. He would have to go out tonight with the other volunteers and join the retrieval.

She turned on the television, where already a solemn young woman was listing the details known so far: a body found by a bushwalker in difficult terrain, badly decomposed and with evidence of animal scavenging. Impossible at this stage to ascertain whether the person was male or female. Local SES on their way to recover the body from the area colloquially known as the Precipice.

Anna closed her eyes and saw the looming cliff with its rocky outcrop and the drop hundreds of metres below. Local people called it the Leap for the stories of Aboriginal families herded there by whites in the early days of settlement. At night, in the keening winds that whipped up the valley, a lone cry from a curlew could sound just like screaming or a baby's sob. How long exactly had it been since she had stood on that cliff edge, half frightened she would jump?

The television showed footage from a helicopter, hundreds of kilometres of bush, mountains and rocky outcrops, hidden crevices and valleys. Anna knew what the search would entail: lines of volunteers in hi-vis clothing walking slowly, side by side through the bush, looking for personal items and any clues as to the person's identity, or evidence as to what had happened. People like her husband, winching in from the cliff top with stretchers ready to haul up the body.

She half-wished she could be there.

'You should come,' her husband said. 'We could do with someone with your skills.'

It was true, they could. But she wouldn't go.

'You know I can't,' she said. 'Doctor said I've got to rest up. Besides,' she nodded to their younger daughter's bedroom, 'it's too late to ask someone to mind Emma.'

'I'll let you know if we find anything,' he said.

She nodded and leaned into him for a moment, nuzzling his neck, murmuring and feeling his warmth.

He sat there, taking it in, listening, nodding and patting her thigh. He was a good man. She waited till the four-wheel drive made its way down their long driveway and was out of earshot before picking up her phone and dialling a number.

'Anna?' a voice answered, shrill.

'Keep calm,' she said. And then she added, 'And keep quiet.'

Two years earlier, Anna's office was successful in gaining a government grant. A small initiative, her boss said at a morning tea to celebrate, but one that could grow across the whole country, benefitting women's groups and raising community awareness of the scourge of family violence.

Anna liked the word 'scourge'. It had a medieval sound to it; conjured images of torture machines and monks whipping themselves. It was a fitting word to describe family violence. They'd be starting the grant on a small scale, her boss said – groups of four or five to begin with, and interested people were encouraged to nominate themselves. The project was a good idea; young lawyers liaising with victims of family violence to better understand their plight. Their time together would be spent in the high country, giving them the chance to immerse themselves in nature, time away from the rat-race to contemplate their own unconscious bias and world view.

This would be facilitated by a social worker trained in family-violence counselling, and a qualified outdoor guide.

Anna wavered with the nomination. Being forty-two years old and three months' pregnant was luck enough – she couldn't risk a thing – and yet her priorities were skewed. Liquorice, raw fish, alcohol, cheeses, all these things she'd mourned but avoided as part of the necessary bother of pregnancy. But a walk in the mountains, the high country of her upbringing, three days on a walk she knew so well she could do it blindfolded, no phones, no iPads, no television, no common luxuries – this she would relish.

She was the perfect candidate for such a project and her boss knew it. Local knowledge, a former outdoor-education guide with rock-climbing experience, as well as a social worker – she could save the company money and deliver a professional experience.

Amid considerable encouragement, she nominated herself for the upcoming program.

The scourge of family violence, a government grant and flattery were what brought her, then, to the beginning of the Saddle Walk, 1000 metres below the summit of Mt Craven in the Victorian High Country on a chilly morning in late February 2015.

With her were two other women. At the last moment, the male barrister from Ballarat pulled out. Remaining were Louise, a young Melbourne lawyer, and Nicole – a woman who could have been thirty or fifty. Nicole's face told a tale of life lived hard. Wrinkles spread around her thin lips and cut deep into her cheekbones like the ancient course of a dry riverbed. A skinny face with dark circles under the eyes and hair limp about her neck.

As part of the project, Louise and Anna were privy to her story: pregnant at a young age to a man who left her; kicked out of home with her son; years spent in sad hostels, where she met her boyfriend Clint Drayson, a convicted criminal who would go on to regularly beat her and her son. At last count, he threw her out of a moving car and tried to run her over. Now, with her former partner in jail for other offences, she was living in secure housing and beginning a TAFE course in

Division 2 nursing. Nicole's personal profile indicated she was hoping to get her life back on track.

But still, Anna eyed her walking partners. Good intent didn't mean good walkers. Louise's pack was too heavy and her boots too new. Nicole looked frail and if she still smoked, then her ability to walk long distances would be hampered. At least her shoes, old Dunlop volleys, were perfect for this trail. The two of them even had jewellery on, earrings, rings and whatnot. They hadn't been prepped. Anna walked the trail in her head: 15 kilometres the first day across the Saddle, then a night in Baynton's Hut. Thirteen kilometres the following day up Mt Craven and down again – to comfortable Patterson's Hut. Then the final day – 4 kilometres up to the Gap and then a final steep 5 kilometres and home to Alpine Valley Road, where they'd be picked up by someone from King Valley's women's health services. An easy trek in all respects.

She checked the satellite phone to make sure it was working and felt her pockets for the spare batteries, mini torch and compass. You could never be too sure up in the mountains. As a child, she and her mother were once caught between Patterson's and Baynton's in a freak snowstorm. They'd hunkered down, built a snow cave and sheltered there till the storm abated, then dug themselves out using a little shovel her mother always carried with her on walks. There'd been times, too, when she'd been called to help out some hiker who'd fallen from the track and needed rescuing. A German backpacker, a child, an older man. These people she'd winched to safety by abseiling down and linking them up to ropes, enabling the people above – or in the German's case, a helicopter – to winch them to safety. Not too many places to fall to your death on the Saddle Walk, but a few. Best to be safe. She'd packed some basic rope gear just in case.

'My phone's not working,' Nicole was saying, walking around and holding her phone up high. 'I left a message for Tyler but I want to talk to him before we head off.'

Louise was leaning against the car, reading some notes from a paper file.

'Not much signal here,' Anna answered. 'And none once we get on the trail. Try to walk up the road a little and see if it works there – otherwise, we have the satellite phone, but strictly only for emergencies.'

'Just like checking in on him,' Nicole said. 'Not really an emergency.'

'Not really.' Anna was firm with the phone's correct usage. 'Try a little bit up the road, it should work.'

She watched as Nicole began walking, head down and arms folded in front of her. The woman was so thin it looked as if a strong gust might blow her off the track.

For the first time, Anna truly regretted her decision to come. Far better to do this walk on her own, as she had in her youth. Young days hiking up here with her two sisters in tow. Hours spent lying among the moss beds and eating sandwiches under snow gum woodlands. They'd almost run the whole track, Anna remembers now with wonder. They'd run along the ridges and into the valleys with little care for injury or safety. How wonderful to be a child in the Australian bush, she thought, before remembering that her own eighteen-month-old daughter suffered allergies and asthma and had been warned against playing in grasses or being exposed to cold air.

Coming up here again was like coming home. The farm was sold now, back to the government as part of the national park buy-back in the early '90s – but Anna couldn't help but believe that the land just north-east of here, the land with the sweeping views of the Bogong valley and of the Precipice to the east, was hers still.

The little homestead, all verandah and chimneys and rooms tacked on over time, had been torn down, the garden her mother planted now taken over by native bush. When they were first married, Anna took her husband there. They found the spot easily enough by the old orchard still thriving among the snowy gums. Crabapples, a wizened pear and two fig trees. They stayed a night in the old house, listening to the possums and bush rats, warming themselves by a fire in the backyard and drinking port from the bottle. It would only be an extra hour from the track to get there. If she was on her own, she could do it easily enough.

Louise hoisted her overlarge pack onto her shoulders and walked towards her. 'It's so uncomfortable,' she said. 'I only bought it yesterday.'

Anna closed her eyes and wished herself away. Already, she could hear the whining about blisters and the delays that would surely follow. New equipment, every guide's curse. She reached out for Louise's pack.

'Here,' she said. 'Let me have a look.' Louise wriggled out of it and passed it to Anna. While Anna undid and redid the shoulder and waist straps, Louise unwrapped and wrapped the piece of paper she'd been holding.

'Anna,' she said in a low voice. 'I've read the latest court reports from Clint's trial – they were sent through to me this morning on request.' She looked up to see Nicole walking back towards them. 'There's a lot in here, but the gist of it is, two days ago they let him out on parole – highly restricted of course – but on parole nonetheless. Can you believe it?'

Anna finished working the straps and passed the pack back to Louise. 'You haven't been in law long enough if you don't believe it. This happens all the time.'

'But he *threw her out of a moving car and then tried to run her over.*'

'I've heard worse. Remember to use your stomach strap – that's the one people forget, and it offers you the most support – takes the weight off your shoulders.'

'Jesus, you're not much of a cynic, are you?' Louise said, half in admiration.

'Realist, you mean.' She was a realist. In her time as a social worker she'd had to take countless women to hospital. Broken jaw bones, slashed faces, acid attacks, violent rapes, and all done in the family home. Nothing surprised her anymore. A dragon could fly up over the mountain and spurt fire out of its arse and still she wouldn't blink. In her job she was known as the practical, responsible one – always capable of making the right decision. After twenty years in the role, emotion no longer clouded her thoughts. Justice did. Doing the right thing.

'Should we tell Nicole? About Clint? I don't think she knows yet – they only notified the most recent victims.'

That's right, Anna remembered. After throwing Nicole out of a car, Clint had gone on to beat up some guy outside a nightclub. The man had to be put in an induced coma. It was that crime he was in jail for, not hurling a woman out of a moving vehicle a year prior.

'So, should we? Tell her?' Louise was hanging on, trying to find answers. Give her a few years, Anna thought. A few years in the system to dull the empathy urge.

'No. Not yet. Let's walk first.' The last thing they all needed was Nicole having panic attacks on the walk, and if they decided to call it off and all go home then nothing would be achieved anyway.

Nicole walked over, a smile on her thin face. 'Got hold of Mum,' she said. 'Tyler's fine and they're off to Ocean Grove tonight, staying in a caravan. He'll be surfing and that the whole time, never mind the weather. Bloody fish, that kid.'

Louise made enthusiastic sounds while Anna held up the satellite phone. 'Well, from now on, there's no reception for your mobiles. Best to turn them off and save the batteries for when we get back in range. We've got this,' she said, gesturing to the phone, 'but as I said to Nicole, it's only for emergencies.'

'Ordering a six-pack of Bundy cans count as an emergency?' Nicole was in a better mood. 'Friday night and all.'

'Not on this walk,' Anna said. 'Let's get moving.'

The three women began walking, specks on top of a mountain range, valleys and peaks engulfing them. Above and beside them was the sky – an endless blue with small white puffs of cloud – and below them a great mountain with a dirt path leading them along the great divide. For an hour they walked across the exposed ridge, sweeping views on either side of mountains and valleys and sky. Towards midday the path traversed through a woodland of drooping gums and the three women stopped to eat their lunch. Louise took off her boots and massaged her toes through her socks.

'How far to go?' she asked.

'About 8 or 9 k's, a bit of uphill,' Anna said, lying backwards. 'Not too bad.'

'My feet are starting to get a bit sore.'

'You've got new boots on. Big mistake.'

'Well, they didn't tell me that when I signed on. Bloody hell! These boots cost $300!'

'What did they tell you? About this walk, I mean?'

'Just that we'd have time to mingle with people who have been victims of abuse, and workers in the field.'

'What, and have a few cocktails and that?' Nicole gave a dry laugh.

'No, I didn't mean that. I s'pose they thought that rather than just being in our privileged positions in Melbourne we should meet people at the coalface.'

Anna looked across the mountains; she hated this type of talk. 'I don't know about any coalface; it feels pretty privileged to be here right now.'

'Yeah,' Nicole said. 'You can keep your dingy city office.'

'And you know what?' Louise said. 'Maybe we don't need to talk about our lives or work at all.'

Anna closed her eyes, felt the sun on her face. Louise stood up in bare feet. 'It's great here,' the lawyer continued. 'I feel like singing!' She spread her arms wide and slowly circled them. 'The hills are alive!'

Nicole and Anna laughed. Louise was easy to like.

'Everything's so green up here!' Louise picked some leaves from a nearby gum and held them close to her face. 'Or sort of green. Olive-green.' Small clouds raced like chariots across the blue sky. A bird circled above. The sun was warm. 'Honestly, I could live here.' Louise gazed over the mountains, picked up the binoculars Anna had lent her and peered through them, turning in a slow circle. 'It's so beautiful. I haven't felt this relaxed in ages.'

Anna grinned. City people always said this when they came here. Compared to the gridlocked roads, the hot alleyways and multitudes of people, the mountains must seem like some sort of Arcadia.

'I really think I might look into real estate in this area.'

'No high-paying jobs, no corporate lunches.'

'Wouldn't worry me,' Louise said. 'Who needs them?'

'Snakes?'

Louise mimicked a shovel-spearing motion. 'I'd kill them.'

'Spiders?'

'Not scared of 'em.'

'Bushfires?'

'Not afraid.'

'Think Black Saturday, Mallacoota – every decade.'

'I'd fight them.' Louise stood like a World War I recruitment poster.

'Well, that's not a good idea.'

'That's what you do, don't you? Communities banding together to fight the flames, blokes in thongs and singlets with a hose?' She was half joking. 'Isn't that what happens? She'll be right, mate.'

'No! Mum, Dad, my sisters – every time there was a fire, we packed up as much stuff as we could and we got the hell out. Bushfires are bloody scary.'

'I don't know. All I'm saying is I could live in a place like this, or in a place near this.'

'Clint used to be in the fire brigade,' Nicole said. 'He fought in Black Saturday.'

The other two didn't comment. Nicole didn't elaborate. Anna looked at her watch and Louise took the hint, pulling her boots back on. They continued along the path. By mid-afternoon they were still walking at a good speed and Anna calculated they'd be at the hut well before sunset. They stopped briefly for a drink. Nicole rubbed her calves. They talked for a while about work and study, listening as Louise told amusing stories about her office. Two hours passed and the women spoke less, muscles beginning to ache. Anna felt more tired than she normally would at this point and she longed to put her feet up. They'd been walking at a slow incline, so when they first saw the man coming in the opposite direction, it seemed he was bearing down on them at a faster pace than he actually was.

'Someone's coming,' she said.

Through the low scrub 400 metres away, the man was walking quickly towards them. Or running. Anna stopped and turned to the other two.

'Probably a jogger.'

'Probably.' Louise looked either side of her.

'Who would go for a run here?' Nicole muttered as they shuffled off the path in single file.

There were joggers who ran this track, Anna knew. Hyper-fit types training for endurance marathons or people on the last leg of their walk who decided to jog the final downhill stage to make the early train from the nearest town.

Red-faced and out of breath, the man raced closer and, once he'd arrived, he paused on the track beside them, resting his hands on his knees. The three women looked at each other over his bowed head.

'You okay?' Anna asked.

'Got any water?' the man asked. 'I've run out.'

Louise fumbled in her pack and passed a drink bottle to him.

'Thanks,' he said, and drank deeply.

'Where've you come from?' Anna asked. 'The Snow Road?'

He put the drink bottle down beside him and spoke without looking up, chest still heaving. 'No,' he said.

'Same way as you. I started out this morning, ran to Baynton's and am now on the home straight. Might be dark by the time I'm finished.'

'With no water?'

The young man lifted his head and flicked his hair.

'Rookie error, left it at the hut. One thing's for sure, I am so glad to see you ladies.' He looked at Louise. 'You on your way to the hut?'

'Yes,' she answered, 'then we're walking the rest of the track.'

'You must be fit,' he said, eyes moving over the length of her frame.

Louise gave a short laugh and Anna rolled her eyes.

Nicole fidgeted with a stick and looked to one side.

'Not too fit,' Louise said.

'Well, we're off,' Anna said. 'Got to get there by sunset.'

The man stretched his calves and nodded. 'The track's a bit run down,' he said. 'Be careful just ahead – that recent rain has really churned it up in parts.'

The women watched him.

'Seen the pig hunters yet?' he asked. They shook their heads. 'Ferals. You know the type.'

Somewhere in a shrub on the path ahead, a bird gave a long, drawn-out cry. The baby in Anna's womb dragged low and deep.

'We know the type.' Nicole was brusque.

'They stab the pigs before shooting them.' The man looked side to side before leaning in. 'Something about the quality of the meat.'

Louise took a step back and Anna cleared her throat.

The man gave a half smile, stood there.

'Well, gotta keep moving,' Anna said before signalling to the other two to continue walking. The women turned once more up the hill, Louise tripping a little in her haste. Anna continued for half a minute before looking back. The man was still standing in the same place, watching them. She gave him a hard look and he gave one back, before smirking and turning around. Once more he began running down the dirt track, away from them. Anna exhaled and turned towards the other two, legs shaky. The women walked on for a few minutes before Louise spoke up.

'Was that weird?' she asked.

It took a while for Anna to answer. 'Not really,' she said. 'There's runners here all the time. He was just a bit of a daft one, that's all.'

'It was weird,' Nicole said in a flat voice that made them all go quiet.

'Creepy,' Louise added. 'The pigs . . .'

The man was right about one thing – the track became harder to navigate as they continued. Recent rains meant it was spread wide and thin, at times veering off the edge of the mountain to the steep sides. The women trod carefully, eyes down, the joy of the walk diminished. After a while, Louise asked them to stop while she took off a boot and inspected her foot – she could feel more blisters. The three of them threw their packs down and sat on the low grass beside the track. The views were magnificent, but Anna knew they couldn't dawdle. Darkness fell fast on the mountain and she wanted to be safe inside Baynton's before it did.

'It really pisses me off,' Louise was saying. 'One weirdo and we're all on tenterhooks. It's not fair. If it was the other way around and we were three guys it would be the woman running on the track who'd be afraid. I mean – why are we all so bloody scared?'

'I've got a fair idea,' Nicole said.

'Shit, sorry,' Louise said, contrite. 'I know you've been through hell with your ex. But why am I scared? The only men I've ever known are good ones.'

'Lucky.'

'It just annoys me, you know? Like now, after that weirdo, I'm always looking behind me – wondering if we're being followed or if someone's hiding in the bushes. He's kind of ruined the walk.'

The other women knew what she meant – every woman on earth knew what she meant. Anna felt a surge of anger. 'Well, don't let him win. We're almost at Baynton's Hut and we'll have a great night. That skinny prick. Don't let the bastards get you down!'

Nicole gave a low laugh. 'I like it,' she said.

Louise gave her foot a final rub, shook out her sock and put her boot back on. 'Okay,' she said. 'Message received. Let's move.' She stood and cupped her hands beside her mouth, calling, 'Skinny pricks in lycra don't scare us!' Her words echoed down the valley, distorted and strange.

Anna clapped her hands together. 'Soon enough we'll be in Baynton's beside a warm fire, cooking up a storm. Let's move.'

They began walking again, somewhat cheered.

Nicole took the lead, moving at a good pace and turning her head sideways every now and then to talk.

She was telling them about her son's schooling when, out of the corner of her eye, Anna saw a black coil thicken to the side of Nicole's left foot. Before she could shout out, the long coil unwound and slid fast across the path, its sleek narrow head darting.

Nicole gave a yelp and hopped sideways, slipping off the path, landing on her backside and skidding down. The others rushed to help as she turned around and continued to slide on her stomach, reaching out, arms flailing and yelling for them to help.

Anna threw down her backpack and, kneeling on her haunches, reached out to grab Nicole's wrist. Behind her, Louise also rushed to assist, sliding on the dirt, trying to grasp Nicole's other hand. In her haste, small rocks from the side of the path raced down the mountainside, gathering speed. 'The bag!' Nicole shouted, but too late – Anna's backpack went tumbling down beside them in a hurl of stones and dirt, too fast and too far to reach. Down it went, leaping and bouncing over rock faces and into the dark bush, far below. Anna swore as Nicole strengthened her grip on the other two and scrambled up to her feet.

'Jesus, sorry,' Louise was saying. 'I must have knocked it and . . .'

'The phone was in there, wasn't it?' Nicole interrupted. Anna nodded. The phone, water, her clothes and most of the food.

Inwardly, she railed. 'Can't be helped now,' she said. 'We've got enough food between us and there's some staples at Baynton's. And at least you've got the binoculars,' she said to Louise. 'I might need to borrow a jumper at some stage, but otherwise we'll be fine.' She thought of the phone and the cost and the pain of the forms she would have to fill out. 'You okay?' she asked Nicole and the other woman nodded, brushing herself down.

The mood soured further, the three trudged on, unsettled and tired. Nicole's ankle was sore; she stopped to give it a rub. The sun sank low in the sky. It would be dark in less than an hour.

'Jesus, what a trek,' Nicole said.

Anna grunted and trudged on.

'I can't stop thinking about that man,' Louise admitted. 'What the hell was he doing running without water?'

'He forgot his bottle, remember?' Anna said, motioning for them to get moving.

Nicole looked up at her before getting to her feet. 'Did he?' she asked. 'You're pretty trusting for a social worker.'

'Why, what do you reckon he was doing?'

Nicole looked at the valleys, silver and grey in the late-afternoon light. 'Oh, I've got my theory.'

'What about not letting the bastards get us down?'

Louise's voice was high.

'What's your theory?' Anna said. 'What was he doing?'

'Watching.'

Anna snorted and shook her head. But she remembered: there had been no other cars parked near the entrance to the walk. A low cloud blocked the sky for an instant and a lone bird cried out. The women were silent. Weak sunshine again. Anna urged them on.

'Why not push on to Patterson's tonight?' Louise said. 'Let's not stay where that creep was.'

'Impossible,' Anna said. 'We can't climb up Mt Craven at night – it's far too dangerous. And it gets so cold here. We'll be right.'

'Besides anything,' Louise said, 'I need a hot shower.'

'No showers at Baynton's.' Nicole's voice was flat.

'How do you know that?' Louise began to walk.

'I've been here before.'

'Really?' Anna turned around.

'Yeah.' Nicole's tone was bitter, and she spun the ring on her finger around. 'What makes you people think I've been nowhere?'

Louise went quiet.

'I came here once, few years ago,' Nicole continued. 'Clint liked to come up the mountains for deer shooting and he took me up here in the early days.'

She grew quiet and started walking again. 'It's one of the reasons I wanted to come here.'

'You want to think about him?' Louise said bitterly. 'After what he did to you?'

'I want to think about what he was like at the start. Before it went to shit.'

'What kind of shit are we talking about?' Anna asked in a low voice.

'Before he started showing us his real fucking colours. Red and black. Bruiser was his nickname at school, you know? I should have guessed.'

'You weren't to know.'

Nicole ignored them and looked around. Looked at the deep valleys and clumps of snow daisies, which hid steep cliff faces. She could remember very well the beauty of this place and the undertone of danger she had felt here. It hadn't gone away. She bent down and held her ankle tight before moving on. 'Clint's a violent arsehole, but he was the son of a violent arsehole too. There was a time he was good to us. I don't forget that. He's in the right place now, though.'

Anna gave Louise a look.

They walked heavily now, distracted and terse. The path grew ever thinner and more difficult to navigate.

Coldness set in. Anna wished herself at home with her husband, sitting on the couch watching Netflix. Louise gave her a spare jumper from her pack, but it was too light, and Anna rubbed at her arms and kneaded her fingers. At last, a hut emerged from beneath a clearing of snow gums.

'Baynton's!' There was relief in Anna's voice. 'Just in the nick of time.' She half jogged towards the wooden hut, before slowing when she noticed that the front door was ajar. She hesitated and stuck her arm out beside her to stop the other women from entering. 'Hello?' she called out, half poking her body inside. 'Anyone here?' A cold feeling came over her and she stood for a moment, waiting.

From somewhere far away a gunshot rang out across the valley. Anna's breathing quickened. She felt the others behind her jump.

Something was not right. This didn't feel like the hut she knew. Taking a breath, she pushed the door further open and stepped in, heart sinking. The others piled in behind her and stopped short. The inside was a mess. Dirty dishes, a chair upturned, a window left open and the cold air streaming in at force. Some crumpled tissues on the floor. Anna walked through to the bathroom, where a magazine lay open – a nude woman with legs splayed and distant eyes stared out from the pages. She kicked the magazine aside and gripped her hands together. She felt sick. Louise walked in behind her and she jumped.

'I can't stay here.' The young lawyer's voice was shaky. 'I just can't.'

'Can't see a water bottle.' Nicole's eyes were darting around the room.

Anna walked out of the hut and took a deep breath.

In the outdoors, she felt better. The other two joined her and sat on the porch, huddled close and talking in low tones. Without mentioning what she was doing, Anna walked up a small hill beside the hut and looked around. The sun was a low red now and the valleys were cast with uneven shadows – black and grey.

Anna circled about slowly, looking towards the path they would follow in the morning and the path they had come from. There was no way they could move tonight. There would be no moonlight and the night would be too cold. They'd have to stay. Get a grip, clean up the hut and stay. She looked up and down the path again. On the Saddle, the trees bent like sentinels and a flock of birds swirled overhead. Shadows shifted, lengthened. She tensed, peering into the uncertain light. Something was moving. Something was passing along the Saddle. She squinted. A black shape, moving steadily along the ridge. A kangaroo, perhaps? But there was no leaping, no detouring from the ridge. The baby inside her moved sharply downwards and she winced. She closed her eyes for one, two, three seconds and opened them again. It was a tinge darker now, but she could still see the sleek figure making steady progress along the flattened path. She called down for Louise to bring her the binoculars, and once they were handed to her, brought them to her eyes, adjusting the focus for an evening sky. At first, nothing. Anna put down the binoculars and tried to locate the moving spot once more. There it was. She raised the binoculars again and saw nothing. Until, finally, she did see something. A figure, human, running along the ridge, a hood covering their head. Wordlessly she passed the binoculars to Louise, who looked through the lenses before passing them to Nicole. The three women looked at each other.

'How long till he gets here?' Louise asked.

'An hour, maybe less,' Anna said.

'Is that a gun he's holding?'

Anna looked again. The figure was holding something. A hiking stick, probably. Probably a hiking stick. 'Unlikely it's a gun.'

'I want to go,' Louise said.

'I'm going,' Nicole declared. 'I'm not waiting around here for him to come back. No fucking way.' She began walking towards the hut.

'Hey, wait a minute,' Anna said. 'We don't know who it is – it could be someone else, some runner, some hiker – someone completely fine.'

'I'm going with Nicole,' Louise said. 'I'm not willing to take the risk.'

Anna thought of what lay ahead in the dark, Mt Craven with its invisible summit and thin, winding path.

'You can't,' she said flatly, 'you'll fall or die of exposure. There'll be no light at all. Just wait till tomorrow.' The two women looked at her. 'Plus, there's three of us. One of them.'

Nicole snorted. 'We going to fight him off? And maybe a gun? Get real.'

The women grew quiet. Anna wanted to resist, fought within herself to resist and be practical and calm, but couldn't. Something about all this felt twisted and wrong. She raised the binoculars again and looked at the dot – now a fully formed figure, running, running along the ridge. Whoever it was, they were moving at a fast pace.

They had 45 minutes maximum.

'Okay,' she said. 'We'll go now – but not up Mt Craven to Patterson's. There's another way. We won't fight him off, or stay to find out who he is – we'll leave. We can take the back trail to my old farmhouse, then cut across the Precipice to Patterson's tomorrow. We'll miss Craven completely and we won't have to deal with whoever that arsehole is coming up this track.'

The two other women nodded, visibly relieved, and within ten minutes the three of them were negotiating a small rocky path behind two water tanks. The sun sank, and darkness descended all along the Great Dividing Range. A deep silence took hold of the three women and they walked quietly – following Anna and waiting patiently when she took time to navigate their surroundings.

This was an old track – there was an easier way to reach the farm from the valley, a steep road winding up the mountain, which led directly to her old place. This was a shortcut for when they walked the Saddle. Sometimes used by hunters and Parks people, but not many others knew the way.

Eventually, the women came to a clearing. The path spun round the side of the mountain and Anna cautioned them to be extra careful. 'Keep one hand on the mountain face,' she said. 'There's ledges, but in places it's a 1000-metre drop.' She kept talking as the path spun a slow wide arc, barely visible in the moonlight. 'Over there – in front of us.' She pointed to an area where the path flattened out and spread into a wide ledge. 'That's the actual Precipice,' she said. 'Years ago, Aboriginal people were forced to jump from it.'

'Jesus,' Louise said.

Anna thought of her own settler background. Of the grainy black and white photos of men standing proudly by ringbarked trees and holding up possum skins. Over the years, her father had built up a small collection of tools he'd found in the earth when digging up the ground for dams and fence posts. Shiny rocks, smoothened and pointed at one end. Another time, a small mound with broken animal bones, bits of an old kangaroo-skin cloak and what was later identified as part of an animal trap. A picnic, she thought now. It looked like the aftermath of a picnic. She imagined groups of people gathered in this area, celebrating an important event.

Her settler relations wrote home to Ireland in wonder at how many of the valleys and mountainsides were cleared perfectly for livestock – as if that was the whole purpose of them! No thought then for the original landowners who managed the land. No mention of the violence and dispossession. The Precipice. It held a fear, the stories of old, and that dark thought that it may have been her ancestors who had done the chasing, the killing. So close in her bloodline.

They trudged on, finally coming across the gates to the old house, wooden and rotting and filled with silver spider webs. Then the house itself: fallen into disrepair and covered in animal shit and dust. Most of the windows were still intact and the old crabapples thrived in the alpine weather. Even those roses that her mother had planted were still there – tall and wild sparks of colour in the green-grey of the bush. She stepped inside and jumped lightly up and down on the floorboards. It was fine. She gave a delighted laugh before turning to the others.

'Come in, come in!' Anna said, waving them through the doorway. 'It's warm inside, come and get out of that wind.'

The three women hurried indoors, shutting the door behind them. Inside, it was warmer and, using a torch, Anna managed to find some old candles left over from her last stay in the house with her husband. Once they were lit, the place became a little home.

'Can we have a fire?' Louise asked, cheered by the new atmosphere. 'How nice would that be?'

'I don't see why not,' Anna said after a moment's thought. The house had always made her feel safe.

Scrounging about in the old woodshed and locating the matches above the kitchen sink, she managed to get a flame going in the fireplace and the place took on a rosy glow.

Together, the women cooked the ready meals over the fire and ate them with camp forks from their packs. Anna made do with a spoon borrowed from Nicole and as she ate the hot food, she felt a sense of relief that all had turned out okay. The anxiety from the track seemed a long way off. They would go hungry without breakfast in the morning, but this time tomorrow night, they'd all be home. From beneath her fluffy jacket, Louise pulled out a small hip flask.

'Well, I never!' Nicole laughed. 'You?'

'Whisky!' Louise said. 'Best thing for pain.'

Anna looked on as Louise poured Nicole a generous amount into a tin cup before swigging from the hipflask. Louise tipped the flask towards her. 'Drink?'

Anna shook her head. 'Can't,' she said. 'Pregnant.'

'Well, congratulations,' Nicole said after a moment of silence. 'You don't look it.'

'And here I am complaining about a blister,' Louise said.

'I'm only thirteen or so weeks.'

'But still, to be out here on a hike – in the middle of nowhere!'

'It's hardly the middle of nowhere. This place is somewhere.'

Louise nodded, her eyes growing misty, and she took another swig. 'I hope one day I'll have a baby.'

Nicole looked at Anna. 'You feeling okay?'

'Yeah – bit tired.'

Nicole drank from her mug. 'Well, good on you. A walk in the countryside like this, reckon it'll do your little one good.'

'That's what I think.'

'See this?' Nicole held up her hand, showing a small gold ring on her finger. 'Got this ring when Tyler turned one. Never take it off. Reminds me of him, you know?' She played with the ring, turning it, rubbing it as she spoke. 'Life may be shit a lot of the time, but it's kids that make it bearable.' She gave the ring a quick kiss and rubbed it some more.

'That's a nice idea, getting a ring on Tyler's first birthday.'

'Best thing I own.'

Louise, still musing about the wonders of pregnancy, began rolling out her sleeping bag and climbing into it. Nicole followed suit. Anna borrowed sleeping sheets from the other two and rugged up as best she could, lying closest to the fire. Among the flickering light of the flames and the sound of the wind against the wooden beams, the women were lulled to sleep. All about them were the mountains, ancient and huge. Cattle, wild pigs, rabbits and foxes roamed, creating havoc with the native vegetation, but the mountain remained and as the introduced species failed or prospered, the mountain would remain still. The women dreamed of big landscapes, of wide skies and powerful winds. Without realising, they huddled closer together, and when they awoke in the pre-dawn, Anna was gone.

Nicole, barely awake, was not worried, but Louise sat up and shone the torch all around. She felt a small prickle of fear and tried to brush it off. Nicole murmured before turning over that Anna was probably just going to the toilet outside. Louise lay still for a moment and tried to relax. Something scuffed against the side of the hut and she sat up, listening. Awake and alert now, she rubbed her arms. It was cold. Really cold. She put on her puffer jacket and found her boots in the near-dark.

Not knowing if the other woman was back asleep or not, she whispered that she was going outside. Nicole grunted faintly in response. Louise stumbled out and called Anna's name softly. Nothing. She tried to peer into the growing light. 'Anna!' she called again, a little louder. There was a crunch behind her and before she could whip around, someone clasped their hand over her mouth. She froze.

'Be quiet.' It was Anna, whispering in her ear. 'There's someone here.' For a moment the two women stood completely still, listening. Anna shielded her watch with one hand to hide the glow and looked at the time: 5.30 am. It would be light in half an hour. She put her face close to Louise's and lifted a forefinger to her lips before pointing to the track ahead that led to the cliffs and then, slowly, she began walking towards it. Louise stood still for a second before following, her breath loud in the still air. After a minute or so there was the sound of a large branch breaking and Louise gave a small scream. A wallaby jumped across the track in front of them. She laughed. 'Well, there you go,' she said. 'There's your stranger.'

'You're probably right.' Anna sounded uncertain. 'It must have been scavenging about the hut for fruit from the orchard. I don't know what I was thinking. But it's weird – I heard something.' Anna stopped talking, didn't mention that she also felt that something was out of place.

She began walking on the track again, trying to dispel the unease. 'Come on,' she said to Louise. 'I'll show you something really spectacular.' Dawn strengthened, and the sky presented a pink and yellow glow. Cushion plants and small shrubs took on sharp silver-grey colours and a bird began to sing, loud and insistent. Louise followed Anna, walking in the growing light to a place where rock, not dirt, lay beneath their feet and Anna stopped, holding out her arm and telling Louise to take care. They were near the edge of a cliff and the view spread out before and around them. The landscape filled their vision and, as the sun emerged, orange and red, the mountains were ablaze with light. The women were silent, and Louise thought briefly that this was one of those moments in life she would always remember. The sun rose a fraction more and the leaves around her shimmered in light and shade. The whole world was taken up with sky and mountain and bush.

'To think!' Louise said. 'This was once your home!'

'Once,' Anna said. 'Briefly.'

She stood. Louise sat on a dried branch from a fallen tree. They took in the view. After a few minutes Anna spoke. 'Better get moving, Nicole might be up.'

Louise yawned and stretched before standing up. She started walking back into the darker trees towards the track, Anna following. A loud crunch sounded behind them and as she turned around, Anna felt someone grasp her arm. She gave a low yell from deep in her throat and was yanked back. Louise turned and stood stock-still in shock as a large man stepped onto the track, grinning.

'Get here,' he said, without letting go of Anna's arm. 'Come back into the light a bit where I can see you both.' He dragged Anna back the way they came with Louise following, not sure how to help. The three of them stood on the rock ledge again and in the light the women could see that the man was around their age and strong. He looked closely at them both.

'Been wondering when youse'd get up. Couldn't be sure if there was a whole group of you in there so wanted to wait a little. Any more friends in there, are there?'

Louise tried to speak, found she couldn't.

The man spat on the ground. 'Where's Nicole?'

'*Clint?*' Louise gathered her wits. 'You're Clint?'

'I said, where's Nicole?'

'Let me go.' Anna tried to wrench herself from the man's grip, but he held tight.

'But how did you get here? Did you follow us?' Louise found her voice.

'Went around to Nic's mother's place to see my kid. No one home, easy enough to get in. Stupid bitch'd written her whole itinerary on the fridge. Hitched here, then got a lift with some old bloke who was coming to pick up his son. The son told me about this group of three women he'd met on the track. One hot, one fat and one ugly. No guessing which ones you two are.' He lost his footing, wrenching Anna sideways with him. 'I'm a hunter – easy enough to see your tracks. Your little fire last night showed me the direction and I found the path first thing.'

Anna thought of telling Louise to run and hide. But where? And Nicole was in the hut, all alone. 'What do you want with Nicole? Why don't you just leave her alone?'

The man pulled her in close to him and looked into her face. 'She's got my kid. She's fucken taken everything.' Clint's eyes were bloodshot, his skin sweaty. His breath was heavy and he stumbled into her. It was a wonder that he'd walked this far. 'Get what's fucken mine,' he muttered, yanking her back onto the path towards the hut.

Anna tried to sit down, slowing Clint's progress and skidding on her backside. 'Leave her alone.' She tried to keep a low voice. 'Just go, get out of here. You're in enough trouble already.'

Clint turned back to her. 'Shut your fucken mouth!'

'Just go now, Clint, go now before this all gets a whole lot worse.'

For a moment, Clint let go of her and, facing him, she backed into the sunlight of the cliff, the rocks hurting her palms. He looked down at her and shook his big head, confused.

'How can this get any worse?'

'You'll go back to jail for stalking, for breaking parole.'

Clint muttered something under his breath and took a few uncertain steps. A bird called overhead and he swung wildly at it.

'Just go now, Clint, we won't tell anyone.'

'Not before I get that bitch.' Clint began walking towards the path again, muttering about Nicole.

'You prick!' Anna stood up and called to him. 'You leave her alone, you arsehole. You leave her alone!'

Without warning, Clint took two steps back towards her, then bent down, slapping her hard across the face. Anna fell to her knees and tried to crawl forward, away from the cliff edge. In the corner of her eye she saw Louise hovering.

'Run!' she called to her through blurred vision. 'Run!'

Clint towered above her, eyes red from whatever he was on. Louise edged sideways, but didn't turn, didn't run.

'What a hero,' Anna said half crying, her head thumping. 'Such a strong man hitting women. You're a loser, Clint, you're a . . .'

'Shut up, you fat fucking bitch.' Clint swung his foot backwards to kick her and Anna grabbed at her stomach, bending down. But before he could connect his foot, Louise hit him hard in the back of the head with the fallen branch she'd been sitting on earlier.

Momentarily dazed, Clint touched the back of his head and staggered before turning from Anna to Louise. 'You bitch,' he said slowly. 'You stupid, stupid bitch.' Unsteady on his feet, he lunged towards her.

Anna scurried away on her hands and knees as Louise stood stricken, Clint bearing down.

'Stop!' There was a cry from the path and Clint stopped.

Nicole stood beneath the canopy of small trees on the edge of the clearing. 'Stop, Clint!' she called again. Louise lurched backward, collapsing on the rock. The sun pierced the clearing and Anna had to squint to watch Nicole. Her head hurt, her back hurt and she couldn't quite believe what was happening.

Clint appeared to relax at the sight of Nicole. His arms slackened, and his red face lit up in a foolish smile.

'Babe,' he said. 'Where you been?'

Nicole didn't move from the shadows into the light. 'What are you doing here?'

Clint shifted on his feet. 'Come to get you, babe,' he said. 'Be a family again.'

Nicole scratched her arm and looked at the ground.

'Come on, babe,' he said. 'Let's go get Ty.'

At the sound of her son's name, Nicole's head jerked up. 'He's not your son.'

From far away, another gunshot sounded in the hills.

'As good as,' Clint said in a new tone.

'No. He's not, Clint,' Nicole repeated. 'I don't want you anywhere near him.'

Clint's face turned a deep red and his loose smile vanished. 'Come with me.'

Nicole hesitated.

'Come with me, Nic.'

Nicole took a step forward.

'Don't go with him!' Anna raised her head and Louise echoed her cry.

Nicole held up her hand. 'Go, Clint, please just go.'

Clint stepped towards her and grabbed her arm, holding her hand to his face. 'You've got that ring on still. That ring cost me big time. It's fucking mine – I told you to give it back.' He pulled her closer towards him. 'Got the car, got the dog, got everything.'

'Don't, Clint, please.' Nicole bent low with pain. 'Let me go.'

'Got everything. You got fucking everything. Give me what's mine, you greedy bitch.' In one move he wrenched the ring off her finger. She fell back, half crying and holding her hand as he put it on his little finger and gave her a wave with it, leering. 'I paid for it, it's mine now.'

'You fuck!' Louise said. 'You got what you wanted, now piss off.'

Clint waved again with the ringed finger. 'I'm not going anywhere. We could have a little party here. I get my wife back and,' he looked at Louise, 'whatever else I'm owed.'

'Don't you touch anyone,' Anna said. 'I won't let you.'

Clint gave a short laugh. 'Shut. The. Fuck. Up,' he said, tapping her stomach with the toe of his boot at each word. He turned to Louise. 'Come closer so I can look at you.'

'Run!' Anna cried to the other women. But before she could shout again, Clint kicked her hard. She felt a sharp pain in her thigh and held her hands up to brace for the second kick. The second kick landed on her hipbone and she moaned, curling down and bending low. As Clint aimed his foot at her a third time she saw a figure flash by, heard a brief yell, and as she looked up she saw Clint falling – arms outstretched and roaring – over the cliff edge.

There was a moment's silence, a suspension of time when Anna and Louise looked at each other, mouths an O of horror. Nicole backed into the cover of the trees again and was bent over, hands on knees. Anna rubbed at her cheek and tried to stand, found that she could. Louise was looking at the sky saying, 'Ohgod-ohgodohgodohgodohgod.' Anna thought she might be sick. She held her hands over her mouth. Her brain was a blur. After a few moments, and beneath the sound of Louise's panicked cries and her own swirling thoughts, she heard something else.

Anna held her hand up for quiet. 'Listen! What's that?'

A strange keening sound came from below the cliff. A keening, then silence, then keening again.

Nicole looked at the others in horror. Anna inched forward on her hands and knees to the edge of the cliff, Louise behind her. Nicole stayed back. Clint was six or seven metres below, lying on a narrow ledge, an arm outstretched and one leg at an odd angle. There was blood around the back of his head and he groaned in that high manner again, like a fox caught in a trap.

'Jesus,' Louise moaned. 'What do we do?'

Still Nicole didn't speak.

Anna cleared her throat. 'We've got to help him. He'll die down there.'

Louise looked at her, open mouthed. 'What?' she said.

'You want to help him? Are you serious? He'll kill us!'

'He's in no condition to do that.' Anna took off her long-sleeve top and wrapped it around her waist. 'I'm going to have to climb down and see if he's okay. I'll try to contain some of that bleeding and then you can run to Patterson's Hut and radio for help. I'll stay here with Nicole, maybe lower some water down to him.'

'No, Anna, you can't. Let's just leave him here. Let's just go.'

'We'll be no better than him, then.'

'Who cares? Who cares!'

'Let the authorities deal with him,' Anna said. 'We've done nothing wrong.'

In the background, Nicole hovered.

'It's the right thing to do, Louise, and you know it. We've got no choice in it.'

With Louise protesting, Anna began the climb down. It had been over six months since she'd last rock climbed – and never on a cliff this high without a harness. But there were ample spots to place her feet, and her hands firmly gripped the rocks. This was what she was good at. She focused on her grip, on each rock in front of her. She breathed in and out, in and out. She chose her footing, felt the rocks firm in her strong hands. She felt steady and thought of nothing else but the mountain.

Above, Louise cried, willing her to come back up.

Anna lowered herself down to where Clint lay on the narrow ridge, panting. He tried to speak and she lifted his head in her hands. He looked like some character from an old Anzac war film, his strong body vulnerable and hurt.

She began tearing the shirt from around her waist into strips to fashion rough bandages. The baby inside her twisted and she held her hand against the movement, closing her eyes for a moment. The doctor had told her she was having a girl.

'You know what will happen, don't you?' Louise was crying now, calling to her from the top of the ridge. 'You'll save him, and the story will be all about him. He fought in Black Saturday, remember? The press will call him a good bloke and all his past charges will be forgotten. They'll say he just *snapped*. He'll be a fucking hero.' Her crying was angry, but she was slowing down, resigned. 'It's you and me who will have to pay for this. You, me and Nicole. He'll come out of it fine, they always do. He'll hurt other women, Anna, you know it.'

Anna rested her head on the back of the ledge. Her head hurt, and she felt a swelling on the side of her thigh. Her whole career had been built on saving people. Social work and rescues – there wasn't much difference when it came down to it. The call-outs, the drama, the danger. She was used to it, used to always saving, saving, saving, no heroics involved. She felt a deep heaviness.

'I was wrong,' Anna said, firstly to herself and then

to Clint. She felt his chest pocket before patting the pockets of his jeans and pulling out a wallet.

'Your baby will be born in prison, Anna,' Louise called through hacking sobs. 'I hope you know that.'

'I was wrong,' Anna repeated.

'Yes,' Clint panted and she leaned in close to hear him. 'But it's going to be alright now. I won't tell what the other girl did.'

'No,' she said slowly, squinting at the rising sun over the far ridge. 'I was wrong about us being no better than you. We *are* better than you. You're a violent, cruel arsehole. You enjoy scaring women. I don't want men like you around when my daughter grows up.'

She put the wallet into the chest pocket of her jacket and zipped it shut.

He looked up at her, at first confused and then with a short shout, comprehending. She shoved him, gently at first and then with her two hands – and then by sitting down and pushing him with her boots, all the while trying to dodge his one flailing, protesting arm. Before she turned to face the sky at the final push, she caught a glimpse of an open mouth, a red gape as she shoved with her boots.

Anna leaned back against the cliff face and watched the sun rise above the mountains. Behind her, the rock was cold and hard. Louise called to her from above and, without answering, Anna turned and began the climb back up. Bits of slate flaked out from beneath her fingers and her mind swirled. One of her feet lost its grip and she looked down to see the bush far below. The rock seemed to bend upwards and away from her. In her head, she saw blurred images of falling figures clutching at rock walls. Time expanded and narrowed. She forgot how to climb. She closed her eyes.

'Anna!' Louise called again, and she breathed, steadied, felt her hands firm on the rock once more.

On reaching the top, she lay down exhausted and peered over the side while Louise paced. Low shrubs and bracken surrounded the broken body, far, far below. The silvery ferns covered it with lacy green and the bush closed in on itself, silent and immense. The mountain appeared unchanged – what had happened made no difference to it – and for that she was glad. She wouldn't need anything more from this place, had no need to interrupt its great beauty again. She would leave it to the birds, to the gums, to the insects and the ferns and the moss. Let the little farmhouse be overtaken and let the crabapples grow wild and prosper. She was done here. People like her were always asking something from the land, wanting it to yield, hide, prosper, enrich. She was done, she would never come back.

Louise was in a bad state, on her way to hyperventilating and clutching her head as if it might explode.

'Calm down.' Anna spoke sharply and in doing so helped to quieten her own fears. She placed her hand on the back of Louise's shoulders and firmly pushed them down, forcing the younger woman to breathe deeply. 'Calm down, Louise.'

Anna felt a pain in her lower abdomen that made her shout. She closed her eyes hard and clenched her fist. She saw red and black and thought she might faint.

'Sit.' Nicole's voice was close. 'You need to rest, Anna.'

Anna breathed hard. The bush seemed to swirl before her eyes and she took hold of the branch of a small snow gum to steady herself. The bush righted itself, righted her, and she sat down on the warm rock. Nicole's voice, when she spoke, was calm and low.

'We can't tell anyone, you know that. This is just between the three of us.'

Louise stopped crying and nodded.

'Clint was a bastard most of the time and the world is a better place without him. But we can't talk about this to anyone, ever.'

Louise spoke up, head still down, her voice shaky. 'On his file it . . .'

'What?'

Louise's voice sounded a little firmer. 'On his file it says he's from North Queensland. They'll look for him there first up. It takes ages to even start to find someone who's on parole.'

'He got parole?'

'Yeah – two days ago.'

Nicole looked tired. 'Jesus – and no one thought to tell me? You do-gooders, honestly.'

'I'm sorry, Nicole,' Anna said. 'That was my decision.'

'Think you're saving the world one poor woman at a time.'

'I'm sorry, Nicole, I really am.'

'It's over. Just forget it.' Nicole shifted on her feet. 'Clint had relatives in New Zealand too, as well as a different surname for years.'

'That's something.' Louise said. 'I guess.'

'We'll have to go back to Baynton's,' Anna said. 'We'll walk on from there. No one needs to know we made this detour. My sore hip is from the fall when we lost the backpack, that's why we took a long time getting back to the Snow Road. We're going to be okay.'

The women stood up and followed Nicole back to the hut, where in silence they began packing and, after leaving the old farmhouse without a glance back, began walking.

The sun's rays caught the whole valley and the trunks of the old snow gums gleamed in the morning light. The landscape stretched on, and when she turned around, Anna saw that the path they'd come on was already hidden in dappled shade. They might never have been here at all. After an hour, the women stopped walking. Louise stopped to retie her bootlaces and as she bent down she put her hands on the ground and let out a small sob.

'I can't do this,' she said. 'I just can't.'

'Yes, you can, Louise,' Nicole said, bending towards her. 'You can do this, and you'll be okay.'

'I want to go home.'

'I know. You'll be home soon.'

Louise rubbed her nose and gave a half nod. Nicole kneeled beside her and patted the younger woman on the back.

'Hey,' she said. 'You've lost an earring.'

Louise looked at her, unblinking.

Nicole repeated, 'You've lost one of your pretty earrings.'

Louise felt her earlobe for the missing silver link. 'So I have.'

Anna, after looking sideways at Nicole, joined in. 'Not sure why you'd want to wear dangly earrings on a bush walk – you lose them, you'll never get them back.'

'Not necessarily. Someone might stumble across it one day.' Louise's voice was flat but she straightened up and started walking.

'Unlikely.'

'But not impossible.'

'Bloody lawyers.'

Anna felt her wedding ring, tight and secure.

'The only ring I ever wore was the one that Clint took from me.' Nicole rubbed her hand. 'He took so many things.'

Anna stopped in her tracks, felt bile rise in her throat. The ring. She clutched the side of her hair and pulled. The ring. She saw Clint wearing it on his little finger and waving at the top of the cliff. Fucking hell! she thought. Why the fuck didn't she get it off him?

Behind her, Louise breathed loud. 'That ring,' the lawyer gasped. 'We have to go back and get it, we can go down the mountain and find the body there, we have to do it, you know we have to do it.'

Nicole was staring at them. 'We're stuffed,' she said, voice rising. 'The ring, it had my name on it, if someone finds it we're done for. I always wore it, every single day. Everyone knows it's mine. We have to get it, Anna.'

Anna rested a hand on the branch of a snow gum and breathed slowly: one, two, three. She thought of Clint falling and the Australian bush covering the body like Caesar covering his face. It was hidden – it was a secret they shared with the landscape. She looked at the other women.

'We can't go back there. It's impossible, think about what it would take. Think about it. It will be okay. It will be okay. Just keep calm and keep quiet. Now move.'

The women walked on. All the things the Clints of the world take from us that we can't get back, Anna thought, running her hands over the top of a soft grey shrub. All the things they wear us down with, the things they hurt us with. The confidence to walk in dark streets, to dance on our own in clubs, to jog when unfit, to fight back, to wear what we want, to say no. All the things they take and have taken.

Louise was walking behind Nicole, babbling. 'Maybe it will work out okay. Maybe it will be fine, and we can all go home and forget this ever happened – and think about it, you'll be able to start again now, Nicole.'

Nicole rubbed at her hand. 'Are you trying to make me feel better, or yourself?' she said.

'You can study, look after Tyler, work and meet someone good. It's all there for you now.'

'Maybe.'

'It is.'

'I dunno.'

'You can do it, Nicole,' Louise said, urgency in her tone. 'Take it all bloody back. Take back everything that you've missed out on. Isn't that right, Anna?'

Anna hesitated, wanting to add something, but she wasn't sure what. She made a ponytail with her hair. Took it out again. 'Keep walking,' she said. 'We need to move.'

Louise looked at her for a long moment. 'So much for the sisterhood.'

Nicole tore gum leaves from a tree and looked at the ground.

'Just get walking.' Anna felt the eyes of the women on her as she turned away.

On the way back, Anna will bury Clint's wallet deep in a wombat hole. She'll burn its contents the first chance she can. Back at Baynton's Hut, Nicole will find a drink bottle under one of the beds and it will provide no solace. Anna will document the lost backpack in the hut logbook. En route to Patterson's Hut, they'll meet a group of deer shooters, four men from the Department of Environment. The men will warn them about a strange young man running back and forth along the mountain path, and they'll offer the use of their satellite phone. At the next hut, Louise will sleep fitfully and won't talk for the rest of the trip.

Anna won't sleep at all. She'll think about the ring. The ring, the ring. She'll try to console herself by picturing the bush and the near-impenetrable scrub. She'll hold her stomach and think of her baby and she'll wish herself back at the farm of her childhood. She'll try to cry and fail. She'll find that she doesn't cry at all. At the end of the walk, they'll be picked up by the women's health services and they won't wave goodbye. They won't hear from each other again.

Until a year and a half later.

When they turn off the TV and before her husband leaves to go and do his civic duty, she'll lean in to him and feel the warmth of his neck. She tells him everything, always has. She may be the best in rescue service for their local SES, but her husband is not far behind. He knows the area well and he'll be first on the scene, lowered down on a winch. He'll have time to himself there, at the bottom of the cliff. He'll need to take photos of the body, the position of the fall. He'll need to check for any personal belongings. She leans into him, and tells him the last thing she needs from the bottom of the Precipice.

THE WANDERER

I'm sitting in the Kafka Oh Kafka café in Prague listening to someone named Wolf talk about the meaning of life.

Wolf is nearing fifty, but he dresses like a backpacker and has the look of someone who's been to one too many full-moon parties. He is probably attractive, if you like lizard types and a goatee. We exaggerate the merits of too many things, Wolf tells us in a low drawl. Places, possessions, clothes. His own sandals, Wolf says, are vegan – sourced from a Buddhist temple in Bhutan where he spent three months praying and working in cotton fields with locals who claimed him as one of their own. He confesses to wearing pants made from buff-tanned red deer leather, but that's only because he killed the animal himself and then ate it raw. He'd been living in the wild for three months by then and was growing weak for lack of nutrients. The small audience nods, transfixed. Wolf tells us that one day when he was travelling through Bolivia, he became violently ill after eating a root given to him by a local tribesman. In the hallucinations that followed, he saw himself as a wandering vessel of sacred knowledge, which is why he now spends most of his time teaching people all over the world about the extreme health benefits of travelling free and living life in the simplest of ways. Members of the audience shake their heads in wonder and a small man beside me begins an uncertain clap before fading off. Wolf says that nowadays he does not eat at all, preferring to derive sustenance from good energy fields and the occasional sliver of arrowroot. There is a collective gasp of admiration and in slow motion a woman near me places the cake she was about to bite into back on her plate. Wolf drinks modestly from a glass of spring water before discreetly lifting a hemp sleeve to check the time.

I snort into my cappuccino and try to catch Rob's eye, but he won't look at me. Instead, he stares at Wolf as if he'd like to take up eternal wandering himself, give up victuals and join the pack. Rob is easily led; he'd tell you so himself. We only came to this café because three good-looking Swedes in Kraków told us it was the best place to hang out in Prague. Out of the corner of my eye I can see people passing around a form to subscribe to Wolf's online teachings.

I look out the window and sigh into my Kafka Oh Kafka cup. Prague is stunning. Like Paris, Vienna, Amsterdam, Berlin and Bruges it oozes that rich history of triumph and tragedy that Europe conveys so well. In Paris, I saw a young Japanese girl weeping at the Eiffel Tower, overcome with the loveliness of the evening scene. Documented by endless selfies, her dewy gaze would provoke the right amount of envy and lust among her followers, making them hate and want her in equal measure. Surely, I said to Rob, selfies are a sign of a civilisation in decline. But Rob is kinder than me. He just thinks that people who take them are vain. He's right about that, but so am I.

Prague delivers that obsessive kind of emotion to some. The place is really something, what with the cobbled streets, the old clocks and the bridges. The walk across the gothic Charles Bridge was meant to be one of the highlights, but it was hard to focus on the fact that it was built in the thirteenth century when people kept shoving selfie sticks into my face. Besides, when you come from a country with one of the oldest continuing cultures on earth, the thirteenth century seems pretty recent. I mean, call me when something really old comes up.

Europe is beautiful, yes. It feels as if someone has wheeled out a new set for us at each turn. But I'm tired.

And sick of places like this café, with overpriced coffee and pretentious staff, the crowds and dickheads like Wolf who won't stop talking.

'Where do you stay the rest of the time?' I raise my voice for the first time and the small group in the café turns around to me in surprise. 'When you're not travelling all over the world, teaching?' Wolf pauses and looks in my direction, squinting. He needs glasses, I think.

Wolf, it turns out, lives in a house owned by his parents. They are retired professors from the Ludwig Maximilian University of Munich. Engineering. Wolf admits this in a louder, faster voice than before, but his tone wavers and I end up feeling mean. In admitting his privilege, Wolf has lost cred with the crowd.

On our way home, Rob tells me off for asking the question. Rob's a friend from my home town back in Australia and he knows me well.

'What's wrong with you, anyway?' he says.

What *is* wrong with me? I think.

'I dunno,' I say.

'It's like you've got to knock everything. I mean, can't you appreciate where we are?'

We pass the old Jewish cemetery.

'Yep, I appreciate it, this place is really something.'

'Look around you, Bec – when are you ever going to get something like this at home?' He points to a woman juggling before a crowd. She's impressive in her tight gold outfit. A lot of people have put money in her busking hat. I agree with him, we would never get that in Pura Pura West.

'We should go out!' Rob's trying to boost my mood. 'Really celebrate our trip, maybe go and eat at that restaurant Anders was talking about – you know, the one where the waiters only speak Latin?'

'It costs about eighty euro for a meal there.'

Rob backs down fast. 'Or, we go to that kebab shop down the road from our hostel, have a few beers, what do you reckon?'

We go to the kebab shop and drink Czech beers while we wait for our orders. A man with a sallow face slumps past us, his hoodie low over his face. A whiff of stale Jim Beam follows him and I wave away the smell as I read the back of his top. *Prague pub crawl – the best night you'll never remember.*

Rob is watching him too. 'Maybe it's a good thing Daniel didn't make it here.'

I give him a look, but he carries on regardless.

'He wouldn't have liked it. Too many people.'

When I speak, I'm angry and my words come out slow and deliberate. 'Dan wanted to come to these places forever. He was always going over maps of Europe, don't you remember?'

'Yeah, but can you imagine him here? Going over that bridge with those crowds? He'd want to jump off!'

'Be pretty hard in a wheelchair.'

'You know what I mean.'

I do know what he means. Dan has never been around crowds like this, not even in Melbourne. But he would have loved all this architecture, all the stories and history. He'd have loved that.

'Well,' Rob paused, feeling bad, 'what do you want to do?'

'I might go on the Prague pub crawl.'

'Not tonight – I mean, after Prague?'

'Vienna, then Dubrovnik, then home.'

Rob goes quiet. 'You make it sound like a chore,' he says.

As a kid, Rob hated our town and left for uni first chance he could. But his studies in agricultural science mean he's always coming back home, working on some new farming technique for his parents. He's been really helpful for Mum and Dad too.

I go quiet. We sit silently in the Prague kebab shop drinking our Czech beers. I think about Daniel in the wheelchair, looking out the window at the paddocks. He was always the farmer, not me. I think about the world map above his single bed, with the red dots on all the places he wanted to go – Paris, Bruges, Dubrovnik, Prague, Vienna, London, Rome.

Later on, the X-rays would remind me of that map, the dots marked out by the surgeon for each new place the cancer had spread. The liver, the spleen, the lungs, the pituitary glands. It was like that Operation game we played when we were kids.

I finish my beer and buy another one for us. Rob's looking at some painting, I'm looking out the window.

I'm thinking of my parents' scramble to try to mitigate the symptoms: the painting of the house to counter the rising damp, the reduction of pesticide use on the farm and the battles with the owners of the nearby pine plantations to halt their twice-yearly helicopter sprays, which for years had drifted onto our farm. While these might have explained the lack of blackberries on our farm, the doctors couldn't completely exclude the sprays as a possible cause of Dan's illness.

At one stage during his treatment, my parents would have paid thousands to fly to Prague to listen to people like Wolf. People who espoused crazy diets, who promised miracle cures if you only listened to them and heeded their words and their wallets. And all the time there was Dan, his wheelchair positioned by the kitchen window looking out at the farm.

It was strange – as my parents sought new ways of farming to try to halt Dan's illness, the land yielded unexpected results. The paddocks came alive with native grasses, plenty of feed for the stock. In the wind, they looked like an orchestra or an audience bowed by a magnificent show.

I think about my father's big farmer's arms carrying his emaciated twenty-year-old son from chair to bed.

Those big, tanned arms with haggard skin from a life lived outdoors, and his son's, sallow and dry, like flaking paint on a dilapidated house. It wasn't right seeing that, and it wasn't right seeing Dad heaving with dry sobs by the tractor later on.

I'm only here because of Daniel. Finishing off what he couldn't start. But it's not me that should be here,

it's him. He's the one who read all the history books –
who knew about the plagues and the wars and the
uprisings and the genocides. He's the one who knew
which writer lived where and what film is set in what
city. I don't know all that and I don't care.

I've nearly missed a whole netball season for this,
I think. Someone else will have taken on Goal Attack
and if it's that Kate Brunt then my goal record could be
in serious jeopardy. I don't give a shit about art.

Truth be told, what I'd most like to be doing right
now is trudging over the paddocks with Daniel, towels
wrapped around our bare shoulders, making our way
to the dam like we used to when we were kids. Once
there, we'd swim out to the old pontoon and dive-
bomb off it all afternoon. Sometimes the neighbours'
kids would join us, but most often it would be just me
and Dan, wiling away the hot afternoons.

Maybe Wolf, for all his adventures, longs most of all
to huddle up in the warmth of his mother's bungalow
in Düsseldorf.

I finish my second beer and grab another. I'm thinking of the farm now and how it's never looked better.
Dan would have loved it. I can't find any trace of my
brother in the Northern Hemisphere. All these places I'm
chasing him in, and he's not here, he's not here.

Maybe in their grief, Mum and Dad have created a place where we can finally see him.

Rob is saying how quick the time is going and that there's only two weeks to go before we fly out. By all accounts, I should be saddened by this. I swig my beer. One more city done and dusted, I think. I look out the window and watch all the people hurry past, a selfie stick or two holding up the crowds. I mouth a silent prayer into my glass: forgive me, Dan. I've exaggerated the merits of travel too much, and there's only fourteen sleeps till I'm home.

A NICE BIT OF LAND

Usually at this time of day Stu is thinking about the nice bit of land just beyond his boundary to the east. Low rolling hills, two spring-fed dams and shady trees. Good earth. Usually he's thinking how he should have snapped it up years ago when he had the chance, before the drought, when the farm was really humming along. But the missed opportunity hasn't made him bitter. He can be good-humored about the loss; these things happen. But still, he admits for the umpteenth time, it is a nice bit of land.

Stu pulls the tractor into line and drives up the next row closer to the fence. The sun is moving slowly behind the trees and Debbie will have the roast on. She'll leave a plate of it in the oven for when he gets home. In the meantime, he's got his corned beef sandwich and a beer to tide him over while he finishes the sowing. Usually his mind would linger on the roast warming in the oven, but not tonight.

Tonight, he's thinking about the party.

Not exactly a party – just a small going-away do at the primary school for the teacher, Dianne Conlan. She's been good for the school, Stu thinks. Patient with his youngest daughter and her reading problems and firm with his son when needed. She's been, as the art teacher said, a real asset for the town. They'll miss her. Joyce Raynor from the post office mentioned it just this morning: 'We'll miss Dianne Conlan – let's hope the next one's not shite.'

Stu left the going-away party before it ended – had to get onto the sowing, but not before he took a good last look at Dianne Conlan. A very thin woman, he reflects. In fact, if he thought about it, he could probably put his hands around her waist and his fingers would nearly touch. He tries it now, steering the tractor with his elbows. Yes, that was about how big her waist was, he thinks, looking at his hands and imagining the shape between. His hands over the wheel look like a pair of puppet mouths straining towards one another. Hello, one hand says to the other. Hello, the other says back.

Stu drives on for a minute or two, thinks about hands. And hair. Dianne Conlan's hair is dark brown, always tied up in some sort of bun thing. But it's probably quite long, he thinks. It would likely reach down past her shoulders and may have some sort of waviness to it – yes, if he was to think about her hair at all, that's what it would be like.

Dianne Conlan. Smart. A dry sort of humour, and not loud or showy. When one of the other teachers gave a speech at the party – long-winded, too many metaphors and references to the old days – she leaned into him and whispered, 'Lest we fucking forget.'

It gave him a shock to hear her whisper the word 'fucking', but it made him laugh too. And there was the smell of her perfume, something woody and dark. Was it perfume? He wouldn't know. Maybe that was just how she smelled all the time.

He changes gears and straightens his course. Bounces up and down a little on the seat. It had been a long time since a woman had whispered 'fucking' to him. It gives him a thrill to remember how it sounded, and he says it again now, peering into the nice bit of land to the east. Kind of funny that the person who said it to him is going away.

Stu remembers six months ago, when he'd been late to pick up their youngest from school. He'd arrived at the gates to find one other man there and Dianne Conlan walking down the front steps to greet him. Her face was very pale; he remembers this. Very pale but determined too, as if she knew what must be done and how to do it.

Something about their behaviour made him wait. He stood as Dianne called out to a young child in the school rooms, who came running and then bounding into the man's arms. Dianne said something low, touched the man on the shoulder and he nodded before turning back to his car.

It was cold outside, but Dianne Conlan stood and watched the man's car drive away. Only when it was out of sight did she turn to him.

'That was Gabe Silva, uncle of Ivy in Grade Two. His sister-in-law's been airlifted to Melbourne. Quad bike accident. Ivy's mother.'

Stu didn't really know the families. They were new to the town from Melbourne, worked from home, had alpacas.

'Do you need me to ring someone? Contact the family or . . .'

'No, that's all been done. I was just waiting for someone to pick up Ivy.'

Dianne Conlan was very still. Stu thought if he touched her arm it would feel like glass. He asked if she'd like a cup of tea, but she said she'd prefer something stronger. He found two beers in his ute and took them into the classroom, where Dianne sat beside his daughter and her own young son on a low children's chair. He sat on a nearby table and passed her the can. 'It's a bit warm,' he said.

They drank warm beer and watched their children draw.

'It's hard to know what to say to someone in a situation like that,' she said.

'I'm sure you did just fine.'

Dianne Conlan looked at him through dark eyes. 'What I said was, *whatever you need, just say the word.*'

'That seems like a good thing to say.'

She nodded. They drank beer. Their children drew.

'I don't think I've really said thank you for all the work you did on the garden beds,' she said after a while. 'The children love them.'

Stu had enjoyed it, digging in the compost, building retaining walls with the Grade Six kids, helping Dianne dig out the roots of an old pine tree.

'It was a pleasure,' he said, and they knew it to be true.

'Will Rex play for the seconds again this week?' he asked. Her husband was a good player when it suited, but too flashy for the likes of Derrinallum East.

Dianne looked into her beer. 'Rex doesn't know what he's doing from one day to the next.'

'Who does?' he said, and she said, 'I do.'

Now, as he turns the tractor around and heads west back up the paddock and closer to the fence line, he thinks of how she said, 'I do,' and he suspects he missed something important, though he's not exactly sure what.

Dianne Conlan. At the going-away party, staff members reminisced about the time she confronted the local member and told him off for not supporting the school infrastructure plan. 'She really gave it to him,' the principal said. 'Wouldn't take no for an answer.'

Stu ponders this, a woman like that.

With one hand he reaches for his corned beef and mustard sandwich and unwraps it, takes a massive bite. As good as it gets, he thinks, looking at the nice bit of land to the east. And then, first in the corner of his eye and then square in his line of vision, he's surprised to see a Toyota Corolla barrelling down the dirt road beside the fence. Surprised and then faintly alarmed because the car is pulling over to the side of the road and the driver is getting out. Stu is surprised because it's not often Toyota Corollas come barrelling down the dirt road at this time of evening, but more so because the car is owned by Dianne Conlan and she's getting out, long legs like exclamation marks, and he can barely believe it's true.

First thought: something's happened at the school, and he turns off the ignition, opens the side door and jumps down onto the ground. But Dianne Conlan gives him a wave and she doesn't look distressed, so it can't be anything bad. He gives a weak wave back and stands and watches as she makes her way across the land.

Decades later, he'll recall her walking towards him – how easily she climbed through the wire fence, lifting the top wire, holding the other down and sliding through smoothly as if it were part of a dance. One, two and she's through. You have to admire a woman who can do that.

He's still holding his sandwich and he takes a nervous bite as Dianne comes close. She's carrying a box – a festive-looking box – and she's looking a bit festive herself with her hair down around her shoulders and her red top bright in the evening light.

She says, 'I was driving to the Reynolds place to drop off their reports and I thought it must be you. Would you like some of my going-away cake? There's plenty left and I know you didn't get any.'

In a rush he tries to swallow his mouthful of corned beef and bread. A great lump goes down his throat too hard and there's a moment of pain that he tries to mask with a smile.

'Are you okay?' Dianne asks.

He nods for yes. Gives his chest a quick slap.

'Would you like some cake?'

'That would be great,' he says, although he's never liked sweet things.

Dianne lifts one knee and balances the box on it while she tries to open the top. It's impressive; he could admire that stance if he had more time. The box wobbles. He steps in, relieves her, and she puts her leg down. While he holds the box, she opens it and takes out a large triangle of cake. There's a moment when he doesn't know what to do with the box, but then he takes a small step back and places it on the rear wheel. Next, he turns to her and accepts the cake, which she's still holding aloft.

He takes a bite. It's a light sort of cake, buttery with a faint taste of cream and something else he can't put his finger on. Something a little spicy. Nutmeg?

'Cinnamon,' Dianne says as if she knows what he's thinking.

He nods and a bit of cake falls onto his arm. He brushes it off, swallows, takes another bite, then another. He gulps down the rest in a rush.

'Did you like it?'

He nods, though he can barely remember what it tasted like. God, he needs a drink. He opens the tractor door, grabs a water bottle, has a large slug. Thinks a moment, then offers it to her. She shakes her head.

Dianne Conlan looks beautiful as she stands beside his tractor. He almost says this aloud but stops himself by feigning a cough. What exactly is she doing here? He feels a slight panic, puts the water bottle back in the cabin. He has no idea what to say.

'How'd the rest of the party go?' he asks after a pause.

'Oh, you know.' She leans with her back against the front wheel. 'The art teacher started arguing with the principal about what flags we display out the front of the school and the librarian read an extract from his erotic novel.'

'Any good?'

Dianne wrinkles her nose. 'Too many adverbs.'

Stu gives a quiet laugh and rests his hand on the tractor wheel so that he is facing her side on. She smiles up at him. He notices tiny freckles across her cheeks, as if a fairy wren with muddy feet has stepped there before flying off.

Dianne turns in the evening light and looks across at the land to the east, the trees drooping shadows, the dam a silver glow.

'That's a nice bit of land,' she says. 'Is it yours?'

'No. But it should be. I could have bought it a while back.'

'What stopped you?'

'Wasn't the right time.'

She shifts, puts her hand on the tractor wheel beside his. Later, he'll recognise it as a brave move.

'You should have made an offer they couldn't refuse,' she says.

He finds he cannot speak.

They look at the hands, one big, one small. Two hands on a tractor wheel.

What to do in such a moment? There's so much that hands can do, they are acutely aware of that – hands are all they can think about – but the hands on the tractor lie still.

Hours later, he'll think that perhaps the thought of the roast waiting for him is what made his hand lie motionless. But that's a lie, he concedes soon enough.

There's the fear of embarrassment of course, the worry of getting it wrong.

Because, he thinks, even in this moment, what if she really does just want to give him a piece of cake? What if he goes to kiss her and she pulls back with a look of horror?

Men have died from embarrassment, he knows this. At Gallipoli, men were too embarrassed to say, 'I'm scared,' and so they climbed over the tops of trenches and were shot with a hot blush on their face. In Vietnam, soldiers offered to go first down tunnels so their mates wouldn't see that they'd shat their pants. He himself had jumped off bridges into swirling rivers because his mates had. He'd shot animals he didn't want to; he'd stood at the altar and said, 'I do,' when really he meant, 'Can I have more time?'

Dianne Conlan runs her hands over her hair and says she should be going. He puts his hands in his pockets, thanks her for the cake and wishes her the best of luck with the future. She collects the empty box from the back wheel of the tractor and walks quickly away from him. The space stretches between them like no-man's-land and it's too late to call out whatever it is he'd like to say. He watches her car drive off into the night; he finishes sowing, parks the tractor, goes home and eats the roast his wife has warmed for him. It's fine, if a little dry.

In the next few days, he'll think back on the incident with a kind of wonder – what had happened, after all? Weeks later and he's still musing over the encounter. Was it just about the cake?

A hand on top of a hand. A word, perhaps; a question? He tries saying aloud the things he might have said. *Would you like . . .?* Too formal. *How about it?* Shit no. *What are you here for anyway?* Aggressive. *Is it only me or are you feeling this too?* Awful! Like the blurb on one of Debbie's romance books.

The nice bit of land across the paddock takes on a new and desperate hue and he'll find that in all his life he's never wanted it more.

Stu imagines Dianne naked. The smallness of her. He probably could have lifted her up, done it that way against the tractor. He closes his eyes tight, remembers how she commented on the nice bit of land and thinks that he should have taken her there. Under the trees, one night by the dam. And what harm would it have done? One night. One hour even and then she'd be gone, and it would be something to hold on to, a gem to give light to the days.

The fact was he didn't say anything, he didn't do anything, and by doing nothing Stu feels his life is altered in some small but vital way.

In the years after, he hears about her from time to time. She split up with her husband and married someone else, had two more children and became a principal. He's glad of it, glad of all her luck and her life. His life is a good one too. Children, a stable marriage, holidays and friends. It's as good as it gets, there's really nothing he could wish for. And yet.

Beyond all his imaginings and manufactured truths, Stu knows this: once, a beautiful woman stopped by at dusk and offered him cake. She climbed through the fence and walked towards him. They talked a little and then she left.

What stopped them in the end? He wonders this for years. What really was there to stop them? The constraints of society, the possibility of rejection, the fear of getting caught. The old human concerns seem petty and crass.

One hand on hers was all it would have taken. One hand on hers.

And even as Stu grows older, when his memory starts to fade after his own wife dies, he marvels that he can remember it still; the way she lifted the top rail of the wire fence as she pushed down the one below, and then one, two – Dianne Conlan was through it and walking towards him in the fading light, her small face determined, his heart an unsteady rush of nerves.

THE ROMANTICS

By the mid-90s my friends and I are burnt out and in various states of backpacker decline. Tired and ill from months of travelling and too many nights out, we lie around in share houses, hungover and broke.

A sprained rib from a mishap in Japan, possessions stolen in Peru, a wound from Red Sea coral that won't go away. We're used to being weak with laughter, but it doesn't seem funny anymore that two Greeks have followed us to the UK.

Rumours that we've turned wild reach our town back home; anxious parents take long flights to issue threats. The act is a wake-up call; we scatter across the globe.

I sign up to a job agency in London, to start looking after old people. I say I'm willing to go anywhere that doesn't involve a flight. That same afternoon, I get a job caring for a woman in a small village in Kent. It's for two weeks and I resign myself to boredom. The quiet nights will do me good. I sleep the whole way there.

When I first meet her, Lady Jane is in her wheelchair, waiting. She has a tartan blanket over her lap and a string of pearls about her neck. She is wearing a white shirt and a purple jumper, and her mauve skirt is long and pleated. Behind her is a manor house three storeys high and acres of landscaped grounds. Lady Jane asks if I'm named after the Queen's sister. I say no, my aunt.

The old lady tuts, turns her wheelchair around, and I think, This is not going to end well.

The first days are long. I help Lady Jane get dressed, I cook her meals, I assist with toiletries.

A nurse comes once a day. At night, I lie in my single bed with thick cotton sheets and I listen to the big old clock, given to her by some cousin of the Queen, going tick, tock, tick, tock. I'm used to stumbling home and sleeping in the same room as my friends or having chats with some stranger in the bunk above. I put a blanket over the clock to muffle the sound but still I hear it: tick, tock, tick, tock.

On my breaks, I walk. At first around the manor house and then beyond, through green fields and woods of oak and dappled shade. I pass through kissing gates and follow old bridleways. Sometimes I weep when I march through the ancient forests, though I hardly know why.

Every step is a poem.

Lady Jane watches me from her window and I take to recounting my walks. We bend in close, we pore over maps, we plot new routes. Over rambles, we bond. Lady Jane tells me of other, secret places she used to go to when she was young. At her urging, I venture deeper into the woods to a place of twisted trees, where an old wooden bridge lies broken over the river. I rest with my cheek on moss and think it's worth it to take untrodden paths.

At night, we read poetry. We like Coleridge and Wordsworth and Keats. Lady Jane can grow confused; once, during Shelley, she slapped me lightly on the face and said, 'Ethel, you're becoming a bore!'

When I wash her silver hair, the Lady tells me stories. She's only ever had one boyfriend and they kissed just once on a rainy beach before he left for war.

She never saw him again.

When I ask if she loved him, she says that she thinks she did and perhaps more with time.

I'm twenty-four and I've only told one person I loved them and it wasn't my family or the boy I went out with for a year. A memory: my friends and I are on the tube in peak hour. Londoners sit like dignified tomb-stones, while we are colourful bats lining the sides. I'm wondering aloud what line Kilburn is on and a young man in a suit says, it's this one, and I say thank you and then I say, good book, because he has rockpool eyes and he's reading *Far from the Madding Crowd* and he says, have you read it and I say, I have. Then my friends and I nudge one another, because he is seriously hot. When he alights at the next stop, my friends sing him goodbye and at the last second I shout with reckless joy, I love you! and he turns and calls back, I love you too! and the Londoners smile into their laps and we in the carriage are carried in a warm glow all the way to Kilburn.

Now, in Kent, I ring the agency and tell them I'd like to stay on. Weeks turn into a month, then two, and when a car pulls up with the Lady's niece and grand-nephew, it feels like a rude intrusion.

The niece is a snob and her son, younger than me, talks only of stocks and property. He is still in thrall to his school and likes to mention parades and raucous dinners. He tells me about all these things when he follows me on one of my walks. I find a massive leaf in the shade of an old oak. I say I'm going to use it as a pillow and he looks at me as if I'm very strange.

I take him to the river and throw a rock in the water beside him. He jumps about, offended and wet. I suggest he throw a rock in beside me to make it even, but he refuses and walks across the field in a huff. His stick figure is bent sideways in the wind as he struggles up the hill. 'Ethel!' I call out. 'You're becoming a bore.'

Talk of property and stocks is the dullest thing in the world. Surely, I think, what is more important and infinitely more interesting is this leaf I hold and this river, this wood. Stocks and property are terrible things to talk about, and pets are the same. Each day the visiting nurse talks at length about her pugs named Rodan and Roxy and I want to stick my head in the oven. And when she began recounting stories about her pets' friends! 'Rodan's poodle friend named Joelene,' and so on.

'I can barely stand it when you talk about Rodan!' I burst out one day. 'Never mind Joelene!'

'Well,' the nurse said, unclipping the catheter, 'you're one for making your point.'

But really – it's of no consequence.

All that matters in the end is surely this: the leaf, the river, the wood.

When the son's figure has disappeared, I find the old bridge. For the first time, I manage to cross it – at first by jumping from beam to splintered beam and then by crawling across the middle part, beneath which the current is deep and strong. While I'm sitting cross-legged on the most solid beam, a white stag comes out of the woods. I hold my breath, suspended, and watch as it drinks from the river, its antlers shimmering in the water.

Time slows.

The trees are silent, the river flows on. Once finished, the stag lifts its regal head and observes me for a long moment before turning back to the woods.

I leap across the bridge to shore.

Lady Jane is the only person I tell.

The next morning, the Lady is in a jumpy, excited state. She refuses breakfast and declares that she wants to go to Pevensey Beach. The niece and I eye each other across the room. It is a terrible day, grey and windy with rain.

I suggest the following week, when the weather will be finer. But Lady Jane won't be dissuaded and the niece, inheritance written over her grabby face, urges me to pack a thermos. To Pevensey Beach we go.

Once there, we sit hunched on pebbles and look out to mutinous waves.

Lady Jane brings up the fact that I used to be a lifeguard. I regret telling her this; I regret it very much.

'At a pool,' I say. 'Not the ocean.'

Lady Jane says that I should go for a swim and that Australian girls are very strong and hardy.

'No one would swim in that,' the niece says.

'An Australian girl would!' Lady Jane says, and I close my eyes.

'No one would.' The niece snaps her purse shut and pulls her scarf around her neck.

Before I can change my mind, I'm kicking off my shoes and pulling my jeans down. I tear off my jacket and lift my jumper and long-sleeve top over my head.

The wind eats into me as I run across the pebbles and into the sea.

It's the worst agony I've ever experienced. The cold mauls me, my limbs freeze and I forget to breathe. When the water hits my stomach, I scream. My teeth explode when I dive under, my head shrinks. Purgatory is ice, not fire.

I try to dive under once more but can't, everything feels strained. I clap the sides of my face, one two three, then turn and run as best as I can back up the beach to the little party, sitting now with open mouths.

The son asks, 'How was it?' and I reply, 'Cold at first, but lovely once you're in.'

When I reach down to pick up the blanket he offers, the son touches the crook of my elbow, rubs his warm fingers there lightly for just a second. 'I thought your skin would be rougher,' he says with a kind of wonder. I flick the blanket up towards me and throw it about my shoulders, but not before I see a mother's dark look.

On the way home in the car, with my head aching, Lady Jane talks of poetry. I sit in the passenger seat, trying to undress under the blanket while I listen to her try to recount *The Rime of the Ancient Mariner*. Inspired by the sea, she wishes to hear it. She prods my arm, asking for help, and after a moment I recite it – the whole first part of the poem. My jaw warms up with the recital. Blood surges through my body; I come to life. When I finish, the rest of the party is quiet.

'Where on earth did you learn that?' the mother asks.

I eye her through the rear-view mirror. 'Honours in English Literature.'

'Impressive,' the son says.

His mother sits back in the seat, sniffs. 'The accent grates,' she says, and in that moment I decide to sleep with her son.

On the rest of the way home, we sit in silence.

That night, I steal into the son's room and sit on the edge of his bed. He's wearing pyjamas and reading a book on historical buildings in Wales. Animosity towards him and his nation fades. I take the book, mark the page he is on and set it down.

'Do you come here often?' I ask.

'I haven't slept with many girls,' he says, which I take to mean none, and his hands shake like a young leaf.

His mother taps on the wall of the room next door and calls, 'How are you getting on in that hard old bed, darling?' He shouts back, 'Mother, I have high hopes,' and we laugh and laugh into the pillows.

Afterwards, we have a cup of tea and a Hobnob biscuit. He tells me he's never had a girlfriend and I suggest that he hold off on talking about his family lineage, or stocks or where he went to school. It's boring, I tell him. Girls don't care about dads who are viscounts.

'Some do,' he says, 'and some want all that comes with it.' Perhaps he is right. But not the girls I know, not me.

'What do you want?' he asks, and I tell him, 'Glow worms.' 'Wordsworth,' I add, and he says, 'Ahhh.' But I don't know if they taught poetry at his public school or talk about it much at his father's bank.

The next morning, I'm up early. I go right around the woods and past the restored church. I sit on top of a kissing gate and listen to the birds. I wait. The week before, one of my friends suggested in a glum voice over the phone that perhaps it was time we should start looking for boyfriends. I kick my feet against the wooden posts. Boyfriends can go to hell, I think. But the thought rests uneasy and doesn't go away.

When I get back to the manor, the visitors have gone and there's a note on my bed, lying on top of the massive leaf:

Australian girl
Doesn't like prissy blokes or stocks.
Only likes trees and walks
And poetry

In years to come, a friend will send me the section of a glossy magazine where his society wedding is featured over two pages. In the background, his mother scowls. His wife is a Kiwi.

When I tuck Lady Jane in that evening, the night is full of silver moon. Lady Jane is ninety-four.

One kiss in all that time.

In her blue night dress in the narrow bed, she looks like a tiny bird. She touches the side of my face with her thin hand and I press my cheek on hers. I think, she's not long for this world.

In my own bedroom, I take the blanket off the clock and wrap it around my arms. I look out to where the twisted trees and river lie and wonder about Lady Jane and her lost love. Three months ago, I would have cried weak tears for all that she has missed.

But Kent has made me a romantic. Now I see glimmering lights everywhere I look.

And perhaps that one kiss of Lady Jane's was worth it, worth all the drunken, glorious trysts I have had. Perhaps it was the kiss to end all kisses. You could live on such a kiss for fifty years or more, it would fill whole days and restless nights.

A kiss on the beach, a letter on a leaf, a declaration from a train.

Like glow worms on a cold English night, we are lifted up, carried along and placed.

We burst and fade, we burst and fade.

RETURN

It was hard to hear Vanessa's voice over the phone. The coverage from his end wasn't great and she was at a champagne breakfast, so there was a bit of background noise. Peter wanted to hear how it was all going, what she thought of his new play and how much she missed him but all she kept talking about was Blinky.

Blinky. He asks her if Blinky's parents are koalas, but she doesn't find it funny. Blinky, she answers, has just been shortlisted for the Booker, and everyone is reading his work. It seems to resonate, she says. People are yearning for this type of thing. Peter has read the blurb for Blinky's book. It's about a retired Cold War spy moving to the Lake District and falling in love with a woman who raises goats. He couldn't imagine how anyone could relate to that, apart from retired spies or goat fans, especially when the author was some sort of weirdo marsupial.

But Vanessa wouldn't listen. She said that Blinky's writing was beautiful, his descriptions of the landscape so evocative that local hotels couldn't keep up with avid readers rushing to find the place where Spencer McLaren first spied the beautiful Maisie Jones and her goats.

Peter holds the phone away from his ear. He can't stand this type of talk and the thought of Blinky makes him want to punch something very hard. Had Blinky cast some sort of stupid spell on Vanessa? She wasn't normally so inarticulate. She must be drunk, he decides, and when he asks her, she says that yes, she is – very much so – and she must hang up the phone because she wants to drink some more.

He says goodbye, puts the phone back in his pocket and feels for the first time the full force of the distance between them. A long drive to Melbourne, a day on a plane and an hour on the tube to Kilburn. Thirty hours, say, not including the wait time for some storm hovering over the city or a security scare. He squints towards the driveway. It was even a good twenty-minute walk to get to the gate. He sighs. 'I may as well be in Pura Pura,' he says in his best theatre voice. 'But hang on a minute,' he continues, 'I *am* in Pura Pura. What a fucking coincidence!'

He laughs a kind of crazy laugh and remembers when Vanessa last called his work beautiful. It seems an eternity ago, but in reality it would have been five years, when he first moved to London. He'd written a play called *Prints* about a dying man looking at photographs of the landmarks that surrounded his home, reliving his past. A low hill, parched paddocks, dank dams and the troubling scars in the canoe tree. *Prints* was an instant success. He won the Australian Emerging Playwrights' Prize and within a week was on a cheap flight to London, economy packed with Contiki tourists, business chock-full with cricketers and ex-*Neighbours* stars, all headed for the Euro dream.

He picks up the bottle of scotch beside him, stolen from his father's house, and takes three large slugs.

Bloody Blinky with his fluffy ears and his big paws trying to write his next book. Good luck with that one, mate. Peter drinks more, imagining what advice he'd give to Blinky if he had the chance: stick to your own country and write about things that your fellow countrymen and women understand. Only the Brits get Cold War spies. And maybe the Russians.

Stick to what you know – isn't that the great tenet of writing, after all? *Prints* was popular among the judges and acclaimed throughout the Australian literary scene. His one success. But he knows a major part of the appeal for the metro critics was his rural charm.

His kid-from-the-sticks freckles and his big handshake – they loved him. And in their pale critical eyes, he could see a kind of longing. In this country, doesn't every man secretly want to be like Clancy of the Overflow? What greater honour is there in Australia than riding down some mountain on a brumby at breakneck speed? What greater honour? He takes another slug, and is alarmed to feel a sob coming on.

Already, he can see that his new play will be a flop. No one wants to read comedies, especially satirical ones set in Syria. What did Vanessa always tell him? Write about what you love.

Suddenly, Peter crumples like a decrepit building.

His poorly constructed self lies shattered on the earth, and he cries. He kicks off his shoes, wriggles out of his black jacket and discards his tie. He lies in the brown dirt feeling the sun warm his face. He runs fingers through the soil and thinks about nothing.

He moves his arms up and down, he digs his heels into the dirt. He makes little castles in the dust.

He rolls onto his stomach and back again, and again.
And then he's rolling, rolling in the dirt, and it's just one
of the best things he's done in ages. His face is dirty and
there's sharp grass digging into his neck and granules
in his eyes. He's flattening the earth, roughing it up,
getting it all over him. His black pants and white shirt
are brown now and he doesn't care. He doesn't bloody
care! He turns onto his stomach, pokes his tongue out
and tastes the earth. It's gritty and hard and it gets
stuck in the back of his teeth. He spits a globule to the
ground and pokes it about with his finger, making a
dark red paste. He remembers doing this as a boy. He
pokes his tongue out again and has another taste. It's
no better, but it's no worse. He lies on his side, knees
up to his chest like a child and once more he thinks of
nothing. He feels the little stones in his mouth and ears
and the sand trickling between his fingers and the sky
is big and blue and the wind is low.

It's been two weeks since his mother's heart attack.

She wouldn't like to see him rolling about in the
dirt like this, but still he doesn't get up. Maybe he is
his father's son after all. Heart attack in the roses as she
staggered out to sprinkle them with grey water from

the shower. Collapsed among the Holy Toledos, the Yvonne Kennys and the Wedding Bells. Years ago, she'd visited him in England, and he'd taken her on a tour of the famous rose gardens of London. Although they'd enjoyed their time together, he sensed her fretting the whole time, for her garden. He suspects that when the time comes, she would prefer to be buried under her roses, making herself into compost for them – but he doesn't suggest the idea. Not yet. His father has taken the heart attack badly. It's a rare farmer who considers the health of his wife before the farm, and now his old man is facing the thought of what the next few years may hold. Like it or not, he's come to the realisation that it wasn't only the roses she kept alive all this time. And that question this morning from the family lawyer: What do you want to do with the farm? The deflated way his father looked at him . . . it's another reason, he admits, why he finds himself drinking scotch and rolling about on the bare earth.

Peter can't decide whether that look from his father is an improvement on the wary one his mother gave him when he visited her in hospital. He bent to kiss her and felt her move away slightly, as if he was being overly familiar. Had they really been strangers for so long? Her hands looked paper-thin and he touched one of them, feeling the dry skin crackle under his touch.

He remembers those hands rubbing big circles on his back to help him sleep when he was a boy. Big warm circles and a half-remembered song about a mouse. In the hospital, with all the tubes and machines, it would have been difficult to attempt a big warm circle on her, impossible really. Instead, he tried to regale her with gossip from the London theatre scene and news about his latest play, but this fell flat. It was only when he mentioned Vanessa that his mother's face seemed to loosen and her eyes focused on him. The two women got along very well when they met in London.

Because, of course, it was grandchildren that she was after, little people running around the farm and feeding lambs with a bottle. 'Wedding bells?' he thought he heard his mother whisper, but he wasn't sure whether she meant marriage or rose bushes. In any case, he had no answer – he hasn't fed her plants the whole time he's been home. He digs his fingers into the soil, he makes circles in the dirt.

A scene comes to him: He's twelve years old and sent to call his father in for tea. He trudges up the paddocks, thinking about the book he was reading, wishing himself away, when he sees his father kneeling beside a fence, tightening the wires. He goes to call out to him but stops when the man drops the tool he's working with, clasps both hands together and rests them on top of the fence. Peter opens his mouth again, but no words come. He watches and waits, half afraid of intruding.

His father is staring across the paddocks, at the shadows widening and the orange ball of a sun descending fast. His weather-beaten skin is golden in the dying light and the expression on his face is radiant. In this scene, his father is not deflated. He is something completely the opposite.

Peter lets this image recede, then rolls onto his back.

He opens his eyes and is horribly startled to see the large face of Ian Drummond, his father's nearest neighbour, looming above.

'Peter Finch,' the big man says. 'Well fuck me sideways.'

'Not if I can help it,' Peter answers, words made difficult by the scotch and the dirt.

'So, you're back.'

'Yep.'

'The prodigal sun shining out of his arse.'

Peter shrugs.

'Been back long?' Drummond asks.

'Ten days.'

'Shit, I didn't know.'

'Doesn't matter.'

'Sorry to hear about your mother,' Drummond says. 'Hope she pulls through okay.'

'Yeah, well . . .'

'Good woman and not a bad sort in her time.'

'She's not dead, you know,' Peter says.

'Would have had a crack at her myself only had Beverley's heavy breathing down my neck for most of the '70s. Hard enough keeping up with her carnal demands, let alone your mother's.'

'That right?'

Drummond points to his gut. 'God's gift, mate, god's gift.'

'Shit,' Peter says. 'Whatever happened to some nice towels?' He fumbles for the scotch, lifts his head and shoulders from the ground like a wounded soldier and has a sip before offering it up to Ian. Ian shakes his head and gives a sideward nod to indicate the stubby of beer in his hand. In rural Australia, Peter thinks, it's sufficient to communicate with nods, shakes and small flicks of the finger. He gives a sideward nod to the ground to invite Ian to sit down next to him. Ian shakes his head. Peter shrugs. The two men drink deeply.

The sun sinks on the horizon. It's orange and yellow and the dams are made into pink shimmering lakes. Peter thinks about his father kneeling beneath such a sky. He leans up on one elbow and takes a risk. 'Ian,' he says more drunkenly than he feels, 'have you ever thought that it's kind of holy, how people feel about this land?'

Ian gives him a downwards glance and burps. 'How the fuck would I know?' he says. 'I'm a lapsed Catholic married to a Church of England sex addict. I'm not Stephen Hawking, you know.'

'I don't think even he'd know that.'

'He knew everything there is to know, mate. Everything. I've seen the shows.' Ian necks the rest of his can and throws it at a mob of sheep in the next paddock.

'Seen all the shows. But I tell you what he might have said, or wrote, or whatever it is he did into that machine. He might have said that we live in a pretty nice spot of the universe. And he might tell us not to fuck it up by being the general fuckheads we are. That's my ten cents' worth.'

Peter is impressed. He likes a succinct argument. But there's a message in there somewhere . . . or one coming. It is. Ian speaks.

'Now I dunno what this rolling around in the dirt is all about, maybe it's some hippie Stonehenge shit you've got yourself into over there, but you might consider staying longer this time. Keep your old man company, help him out a bit. He's not getting any younger and there's only so many times I can drive over to show him how to use the new pump. Stay. You can do more of your rolling around. Even give the seconds a shot.'

Peter remembers playing football, all that half-hearted dancing around the pack and the fumbled marks. 'They wouldn't have me,' he says. 'Not even in the seconds.'

'You're right. They're only bottom of the ladder, not terminal. Well, come and be a water boy if it's not too much trouble for a Pommy dickhead like your fine self.'

'I'll think about it.'

'And, for Chrissake, get rid of the black suit. You look like some sort of shithouse spy.'

Ian nods down at him and Peter nods up at him.

Then the big man walks off, heading towards the house, giving a backwards wave with his big meaty hand. Peter rests one cheek in the dirt and watches till his father's friend is a black speck shimmering in the heat.

What do you want to do with the farm?

He thinks about growing up and the old black and white photos of his family members and the stories of droughts and fires and locusts. He thinks about his parents telling him to stop reading and to help with the drenching, the shearing, the lambing and the fencing.

He thinks about the fact that he's an only child. He thinks about all that bullshit about his great-great-grandfather settling the land and clearing it and making it profitable, about his great-grandfather building the house and raising the money for the little bush school.

All the bullshit that ignored the scars in the canoe trees and the perfect rocks smoothed into carved edges that the header sometimes pulled up. All that ignorant white bullshit that he scorned in Melbourne and London and that now he couldn't ignore and yet couldn't reject outright.

He didn't want the farm, didn't want it, didn't want it! And yet, now, he does. This farm, this land, the brown soil, he wants to be part of it. He's tired of resisting the urge and tired of travelling, which surely is another word for escape. He could live here on the farm with his old man and help out, learn about the seasons, grow some more trees. Despite what the doctors say, his mother could pull through and he could help her run the place, build a watering system for the roses and whatnot. He could come up here and lie like this, think about another play. Vanessa could hang up her high heels, move here and try her hand at farming – well, why not? He could try to find out who lived on this land before his great-great-grandfather and what they did.

Forget his equine allergy, he could learn to ride a horse!

It could work, it could all work.

Finally, as night closes in over the paddocks, he thinks of Blinky and how perhaps Vanessa was right. That a man, an object of suspicion and fear, a man brought in from the cold to warmth and beauty and love might indeed be a story worthy of merit. As a fiction, it might even be beautiful.

ACKNOWLEDGEMENTS

Thank you to the friends who provide honest commentary on my work. They are firefighters and artists and engineers and farmers and welders and teachers and climate experts and academics and it's people like them who make living in the country great.

I am grateful to Drs Jennifer Jones and Sue Gillett from La Trobe University who offered excellent advice throughout my studies.

Thank you to MidnightSun Publishing for publishing the first edition of *Rural Dreams*, and a massive thanks to Beverley Cousins, Holly Toohey, Melissa Lane and Jodie Ramodien for bringing it to new life at Penguin

Books Australia. Thanks also to Christa Moffitt for the beautiful cover.

Always and most of all, thanks to Alexander, Eddie, Ben and Bern.

AUTHOR'S NOTE

This collection was written on the lands of the Waywurru and Dhudhuroa peoples, whom I would like to acknowledge as the Traditional Custodians and Storytellers of their country. I pay my respects to their Elders past and present, and celebrate all the histories, traditions and living cultures of Aboriginal and Torres Strait Islander people.

Two stories in *Rural Dreams* have been published previously as monologues. 'Coach' and 'Twitcher' were published in *Bloke* by Playlab Indie. Some stories have been published in journals and anthologies: 'Saturday Morning' appeared in *Meanjin*, 'The Romantics' was published in the *Newcastle Short Story Award*

Anthology 2020 and 'Glory Days' was included in *ACE: Arresting, Contemporary Stories from Emerging Writers*. 'A Nice Bit of Land' is a new addition to this collection, and was first published in *Island* magazine. Several stories have won or been shortlisted for awards and a number of them first appeared in the creative component of my PhD. 'The Precipice' was the basis for my novel *The Creeper*.

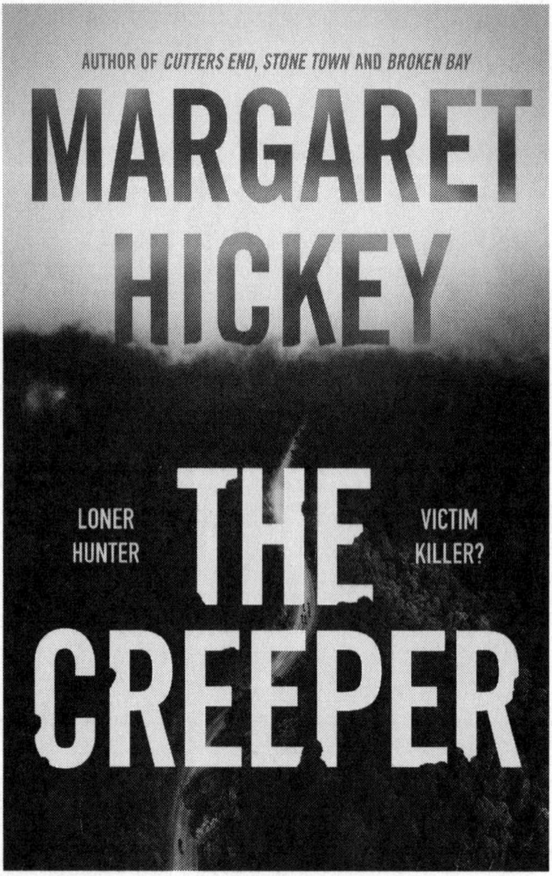
AUTHOR OF CUTTERS END, STONE TOWN AND BROKEN BAY
MARGARET HICKEY
LONER
HUNTER
VICTIM
KILLER?
THE CREEPER

THE CREEPER
Margaret Hickey

For the last decade, the small mountain town of Edenville in Victoria's high country has been haunted by the horrific murders of five hikers up on Jagged Ridge.

Also found dead near the scene was Bill 'Creeper' Durant, a bushland loner, expert deer-hunter, and a man with a known reputation for stalking campers . . .

Conclusion: murder-suicide. Case closed.

But as the ten-year anniversary of the massacre draws near, Detective Constable Sally White – the only officer at Edenville's modest police station – finds herself drawn into the dark world of the notorious Durant family.

Lex Durant, in particular, has started to publicly protest his brother's innocence and accuse the police of persecution.

As Sally combs the investigation to prove him wrong, it becomes all too clear that each murdered hiker had skeletons in their closet – and possible enemies in their past . . .

Read on for an extract.

PROLOGUE

'Tom, are we lost?'

No answer.

'Tom!'

He was looking at the map again, head close to it, a thin line of sweat running down the back of his neck.

Laura took her pack off and slumped to the ground. Immediately, ants converged, and with a heavy sigh she got up and stumbled to a fallen log. *Let spiders come and bite me*, she thought, sitting down. *I don't give a rat's.* She had a drink of water, then felt about in her pack for a muesli bar.

The sun was fast losing its warmth. Through the steep valleys and ridges of Mount Razor, shadows crept closer.

'I'm getting a blister,' Laura moaned. She took her boot off and inspected her heel. 'Have you got a Band-Aid?'

He still didn't answer, and when she looked up at him again, she saw he had the compass out. For the first time in two days, Laura felt a prickle of alarm.

'Tom. *Are we lost?*'

Her boyfriend put down the map and stared at her. 'I think we missed the turn-off to the campsite. Remember the sign we passed about an hour ago? We should have gone left rather than right.'

'Bloody hell!' she exploded. 'You said you knew where we were going!'

Tom began folding the map back up. 'We'd better get moving, it's getting dark.'

Laura shook her head and rubbed her foot again. Honestly, she might break up with him after this. What was the point of having a boyfriend who said he loved the outdoors when every time he was outside, he got fucking lost? She shook her sock out and put it back on.

He'd been pretty annoying this whole hiking trip, actually. Going on about how she shouldn't have worn new boots for the walk, and how noisy her sleeping mat was. *I mean, shoot me*, she thought. *So I want to be comfortable.* And that English accent she'd found so charming at first was now just plain irritating.

As she pulled her boot on, she felt a shadow pass over, casting everything one shade darker. It wouldn't be long before they needed headtorches. And, just to make matters worse, she felt a cold drop of rain on her face. Zipping up her backpack, she stood.

'Hurry, Laura,' Tom said. 'And don't forget your water bottle.'

Hurry, Laura, she mimicked to herself, but as she leaned over to pick it up, the bottle rolled a short distance down the hill before stopping at a large rock shelf.

'Leave it,' Tom said, 'we've got to get moving.'

'Are you kidding?' Laura was already sliding carefully down the slope. 'Those drink bottles are, like, twenty bucks. And it's just here.'

Something in the corner of her eye made her start: a dark figure, kneeling beside the rock. For a few beats she stood stock still, until the realisation hit that it was a wallaby.

'Oh god!' she called out to Tom. 'I just got the fright of my life!'

Tom muttered something in reply.

'What's that?' she answered, as she retrieved her bottle.

'Be *quiet.*' Tom's voice was sharp.

Laura edged up the slope.

'Can you hear something?' He helped her back onto the rocky path.

'No.'

His face was taut with concentration. 'I thought I heard something – further up the path.'

Laura felt a twist in her gut. It really was getting dark now. 'It's nothing. Come on.'

They started walking.

'There it is again.' Tom turned abruptly. 'Listen.'

Laura stopped. Silence. Then, on the ridge behind them, maybe five hundred metres away: a movement. Something making its way towards them. She narrowed her eyes along the ridge path. Yes – she could make out a definite shape.

'A kangaroo?' she said after a pause.

Tom hesitated, gave a short nod, and then began walking back the way they'd come. She followed, faster now. Yes, it had most definitely been a kangaroo.

Her foot began rubbing again. 'Tom, I seriously need a Band-Aid.'

'Really?' he said. 'Can't it wait?'

'No, it—'

A scream sliced through the air.

Tom and Laura stared at one another, then looked behind them.

The dark shape was now taking human form, running – or limping – towards them through the snow gums on the winding path. Three hundred metres away.

Tom dropped his backpack and began rummaging through it. 'Binoculars,' he said, and handed them to Laura. 'You can see better than me.'

Laura held them up to her eyes, adjusted the setting. The sky was a deep velvet, merging into black. It was difficult to see. But yes, she was sure it was a person. She magnified her view.

A young woman was running, mouth open, glancing behind her, and at the same time pushing forward in their direction. Was that blood across her face?

Laura lowered the binoculars. 'I think she's injured, but I'm not sure.'

'What's she running from?' Tom asked.

Another scream, and this time the words rang through the night, echoing up and down the deep valleys and jagged plains.

Help!

He's coming!

They're all dead.

CHAPTER 1

'For weeks, Australia was fixated by the image: a beautiful woman, running screaming through the bush at night. What occurred in the remote mountainous region of North-East Victoria dominated every TV news program, every magazine and newspaper. What police found shocked the nation . . .'

The reporter on the screen was walking through dry bushland, hair perfect, face solemn. He looked like a Ken doll. Sally sniggered at his tight suit pants and jacket, so unsuitable for the environment. *This reporting is crap*, she thought. *I should switch it off. I really should.*

She turned up the volume.

'One body, lying mangled in the bush, hacked to death. Four more fatally shot. The Parks Victoria officer, local James Brear . . .'

'Jim!' Sally called. 'Get in here, you're on the telly!'

'. . . who was first on the scene, reported a fox already sniffing at the site.'

Sally sat back. The mention of the fox was a bit too much, bordering on the macabre. Yet she knew viewers would love the grisly detail. Plus, it was true: Jim had told her about the animal on one of the rare occasions he spoke about that day. *The fox,* he kept saying, *it didn't leave, even when I tried to shoo it away. It just stared at me.*

The television screen was now filled with images of the people who had died that night, and then a map of the bush terrain in which they'd been found.

Sally stood up, did a couple of lunges, stretched her calves. It was important to stay fit: one demand of her job she liked. Outside, thick gum trees, closely set, dripped with last night's rain. The air was heavy with it, even indoors. And to the back of the bush, Mount Razor rose like a god, its peak invisible in the cloudy morning air. Water would be cascading down its gigantic boulders; lacy ferns would droop like ballerina hands; and creatures would take cover in logs, burrows and caves. Everything bowed towards the mountain around here, the people most of all.

Sally called out to Jim again before dropping down to a plank position. She was trying to plank each morning for five minutes; it was excellent for the core. The report turned to early footage once more; this time, the police commissioner and a family member were being interviewed.

Barely kilometres from where she was planking right now, Sally thought, as her gut tightened and her breathing became laboured. A massacre just up the road.

'And now, ten years on, the sole survivor, Laura Wynter, has finally agreed to talk about what happened that night. Her story, her words. Catch our exclusive on the Mountain Murders on—'

'Why are you even watching this?'

Sally started, she hadn't heard Jim come in. Her plank wobbled.

'It was just on.' She gave up the position and lay on her side. 'I thought you'd be interested.'

'I am not one bit interested.' He was staring at the screen.

'Well, like it or not, it's about to blow up.' Sally glanced at her boyfriend. 'Ten-year anniversary.'

Jim made a *humph* sound, walked to the fridge, and took a long look inside. 'I hate the way they're going to rake it up. You weren't here when it happened, Sal. You don't know what it was like for everyone.'

Sally went quiet. The reason she didn't know was because he barely talked about what he'd seen that day.

Jim rustled about in the fridge and selected a large apple. 'I wonder why she's talking now,' he said to the piece of fruit. He was referring to the beautiful woman whose face was plastered across the screen. *Sole survivor.*

Ten years ago, in the dark of night, Jim had carried Laura Wynter to safety, fifteen kilometres through rough terrain on the Razor. *What does that do to a person?* Sally wondered, not for the first time.

'I'd say a million dollars is why she's talking now.' Sally didn't like the peevish tone that had crept into her voice. 'Wouldn't you?'

Jim nodded and walked past her, touching her absentmindedly on the shoulder. 'Probably,' he said.

As he headed outside to his Parks Victoria ute, she knocked on the kitchen window and he turned around. She gave him a heart sign with her hands. He gave it back. They did it jokingly, of course, but it made her feel better.

Sally's eyes turned back to the screen, where the reporter was now kneeling by a small marker, touching it reverently, closing his eyes. She knew that marker, had read it a dozen times when she'd been walking along the Razor track.

In memory of the five hikers who tragically lost their lives on this trail
24th February 2014
Brooke Arruda
Kate Barone
Tom Evans
Lyn Howlett
Russell Walker

Five hikers. The sign didn't include the local deer hunter, who was charged with murder-suicide. He didn't rate a mention. Bill Durant: known as Deer Man to some; The Creeper to others. It was only recently, now the anniversary loomed, that Sally was beginning to hear his real name spoken.

Senior Constable Sally White picked up her keys and, after locking the house, climbed into her work-issued Toyota and drove the short distance to the police station. She passed one car on the way, gave the driver a toot: it was Don from up the road. Sally liked Don. He brought her tomatoes from his garden and gave her advice on the best walking tracks. Two months ago, she and Don had pushed a barrow full of zucchinis all the way up the Razor for charity. The man was nearing eighty, but he could walk like nobody's business.

She drove over the Garrong River bridge, noting the rising swell of water beneath. Among other things to do today, she'd have to check the weather reports – road closures over Clearcut Creek might be necessary. For now, the sun shone through the clouds. A good song was playing on the radio: 'Lazy Eye' by Silversun Pickups. She turned up the volume and sang the tune out loud, beating her hands against the wheel as she made a sharp left down a dirt road and then a sharp right into the main street of Edenville.

Sally killed the engine, but not the song; she sat in the police car singing along. It was Thursday morning, all quiet in town. Stone gutters gushed with leaves and water; footpaths glistened; trees bent low. Despite the summer month, everything was lush and green. Six months into her work here, and Sally still marvelled at her luck: a posting in a mountain town, a hot boyfriend, good people and valleys and rivers and waterholes and country pubs. It was a world away from her Adelaide upbringing, then boarding school in Melbourne, flitting between the cities like a migrating bird.

People always talked about the death of small country towns, but it wasn't the case here – no siree, it was not. The whole town glistened with newfound wealth. New businesses were setting up in the main street: a wholefood store, a wine bar scheduled to open in weeks. Old weatherboards lining the river were being torn down and rebuilt in handsome wood and steel; enormous windows with views of the mountains and the sky. House prices were edging past a million; rents were soaring. It was pricy here in Edenville, but ah, what wealth could do! She looked with pride at the maple-lined streets and evergreen poplars. For the tourists, tree-changers and grey nomads, Edenville was a shiny Christmas present under the tree.

The song ended with a steady beat then a high thrum. Sally pulled her long blonde hair into a ponytail, briefly checked the mirror and stepped out of the car, ripping up a few weeds as she walked into Edenville police station. It was a pretty building, like something from a children's book: white weatherboard, roses and geraniums. Add that to the list of good things about her life: a picturesque police station all to herself. Her friends in the city worked in offices where they were crammed two to a desk; it was like dodgem cars, they said. You bumped shoulders every time you reached for your half soy. And that reminded her: Corina and Jac, two friends from school, were coming up tomorrow night. She whistled a bright tune. Fun times ahead.

Inside, the phone was ringing. Sally picked it up, put on her good voice.

'Senior Constable Sally White speaking, Edenville Police.'

'Seen the news?'

'Is that you, Lex?' Sally's heart sank. The gravelly voice was that of Lex Durant, younger brother of the deceased deer hunter accused of the Mountain Murders.

'Need to speak with you today.'

'Can you come into the station, Lex?'

'Can't. Foot got caught in a rabbit trap. Can't do nothing for a week.'

Rabbit traps were illegal. She'd told him that before.

'Have you been to the clinic about it?'

'Yeah, nurse give me some tablets. Done nothing.'

A young mother walked past the station door, two little children in tow. They looked like something from a 1950s poster, till one of the kids kicked the other hard up the bum. The younger one wailed.

'So, can you come here?' Lex repeated.

The mother handed the screaming child a ball, and the noise stopped instantly.

'No, Lex. You'll need to come to the station.'

There was a pause.

'I'll put the dogs on a chain.'

During her first week in Edenville, she'd been called out to a disturbance on the Durant property. Illegal burning. As soon as she'd climbed out of the police vehicle, three dogs had rushed her, scaring her to death.

Lex's property was down a dirt road on the outskirts of town, situated at the foot of the Razor. The mountain's shadow often covered it in a dark shroud, as if the house was in mourning, and kneeling before a giant. In the near darkness, the old weatherboard structure had had a definite *Wolf Creek* vibe.

Lex cleared his throat down the line. 'Got something to tell you. About my brother.'

A twinge of interest. Sally stretched her calves as she stood. 'Yeah?'

'You should come around.'

Lex had something to say about Bill Durant, did he? The whole country wanted to know about The Creeper right now. Sally looked at her day's schedule. It was relatively free. She made a show of shuffling papers and muttering about work.

'Okay, Lex, I can fit it in. I'll be there just after one.'

The weak ray of sunlight beaming on her desk strengthened, then faded. Maybe it was a sign, Sally thought, before hanging up and turning to her work. Her friend Amelia paid a lot of attention to 'signs'; and not just the run-of-the-mill, black-cat-crossing-your-path kind of stuff. Amelia thought that if someone offered you an orchid at a party, you would die before midnight. But Amelia smoked a lot of weed. So.

Sally looked up the growing list of road closures and made some calls. A woman came in, asking her to sign passport photos. Someone else dropped an eighteenth birthday party invitation on the desk, suggesting she check it out this Saturday night, because it could get wild. Sally noted it all down, then headed off to investigate the state of the roads. *What's a wild eighteenth look like these days?* she wondered. At hers, she'd played beer pong with her mates, then hit the clubs. She'd kissed someone from Ballarat before stumbling back to her share house, her hangover hours away, the sun rising over the bay, and her high heels clicking in her hands.

At the Garrong bridge leading out of town, a Vic Roads worker was already setting up detour signs. The river wasn't yet at flood status, he informed her, but if there was more heavy rain, they'd be closing the road altogether. The worker and Sally both raised their faces to the overcast sky.

'Hang on, won't that cut the town off?' Sally felt a sudden pang of alarm. What about her friends coming from Melbourne?

'Don't worry, town'll be safe as houses,' the worker said, chewing gum loudly.

Sally took out her phone, noted it down. If the town was closed off, she'd have to let the school know, call the larger station in Wexton, check what the full procedure was.

But now, a different emotion – a slight excitement – bubbled up. The town cut off, and her in *actual charge*?

CUTTERS END
Margaret Hickey

**A desert highway. A remote town.
A murder that won't stay hidden.**

New Year's Eve, 1989. Eighteen-year-old Ingrid Mathers is hitchhiking her way to Alice Springs. Bored, hungover and separated from her friend Joanne, she accepts a lift to the remote town of Cutters End.

July 2021. Detective Sergeant Mark Ariti is seconded to a recently reopened case, one in which he has a personal connection. Three decades ago, a burnt and broken body was discovered in scrub off the Stuart Highway, 300 km south of Cutters End. Though ultimately ruled an accidental death, many people – including a high-profile celebrity – are convinced it was murder.

When Mark's interviews with the witnesses in the old case files go nowhere, he has no choice but to make the long journey up the highway to Cutters End.

And with the help of local Senior Constable Jagdeep Kaur, he soon learns that this death isn't the only unsolved case that hangs over the town . . .

**WINNER OF 2022 THE DANGER PRIZE
SHORTLISTED FOR THE 2022 NED KELLY
AWARD FOR FIRST FICTION**

'Astonishingly assured crime debut. A pitch perfect outback noir, set against a vivid and atmospheric desert landscape . . . The book's explosive finale will linger with you for days.' *Weekend Australian*

STONE TOWN
Margaret Hickey

With its gold-rush history long in the past, Stone Town has seen better days. And it's now in the headlines for all the wrong reasons . . .

When three teenagers stumble upon a body in dense bushland one rainy Friday night, Senior Sergeant Mark Ariti's hopes for a quiet posting in his old home town are shattered. The victim is Aidan Sleeth, a property developer, whose controversial plan to buy up local land means few are surprised he ended up dead.

However, his gruesome murder is overshadowed by a mystery consuming the entire nation: the disappearance of Detective Sergeant Natalie Whitsed.

Natalie had been investigating the celebrity wife of crime boss Tony 'The Hook' Scopelliti when she vanished. What did she uncover? Has it cost her her life? And why are the two Homicide detectives, sent from the city to run the Sleeth case, so obsessed with Natalie's fate?

Following a late-night call from his former boss, Mark is sure of one thing: he's now in the middle of a deadly game . . .

'An impressive piece of crime fiction, with good characters, a twisty plot and crisp descriptions of an outback town undergoing change.' *Canberra Weekly*

BROKEN BAY
Margaret Hickey

Old loyalties and decades-long feuds rise to the surface in this stunning crime novel, set in a spectacular Australian landscape known for its jagged cliffs and hidden caves.

Detective Sergeant Mark Ariti has taken a few days' holiday in Broken Bay at precisely the wrong time. The small fishing town on South Australia's Limestone Coast is now the scene of a terrible tragedy.

Renowned cave diver Mya Rennik has drowned while exploring a sinkhole on the land of wealthy farmer Frank Doyle. As the press descends, Mark's boss orders him to stay put and assist the police operation.

But when they retrieve Mya's body, a whole new mystery is opened up, around the disappearance of a young local woman twenty years before . . .

Suddenly Mark is diving deep into the town's history – and in particular the simmering rivalry between its two most prominent families, the Doyles and Sinclairs.

Then a murder takes place at the Sinclairs' old home – and Mark is left wondering which is more dangerous: Broken Bay's hidden subterranean world or the secretive town above it . . .

'This is the third novel featuring Detective Mark Ariti, and a ripper it is too . . . A fabulous addition to the wealth of Bush Noir novels available, and I recommend it highly.' *Good Reading*

Powered by Penguin

Looking for more great reads, exclusive content and book giveaways?

Subscribe to our weekly newsletter.

Scan the QR code or visit penguin.com.au/signup